"Maybe it isn't a good idea for you to fraternize with the enemy."

Michael shook his head. "I have to take issue with that comment."

"Look, Michael—"

The rest of Sam's reply never made it past her lips. Michael cut it off when he framed her face in his hands and leaned in to cover her mouth with his. The encounter was infused with all the passion and promise she remembered so vividly, though she'd done everything during the past seven years to forget it. They were both breathing hard and heavily when Michael pulled away. Afterwards, they stared at one another in stunned silence.

"Wow," Sam murmured.

"Exactly." Though Michael appeared to be just as dazed as she was, he also looked pleased. He touched her lips with the tip of one finger. "Now, *that's* what's called fraternizing with the enemy."

Dear Reader

The idea for this book came in the middle of the night. I got out of bed, jotted down some notes, and was pleasantly surprised when they made sense in the morning. Believe me, that's not always the case.

I imagined an intense rivalry between two advertising executives working in glamorous Manhattan. To complicate matters, I made them former lovers who are trying to land the same huge advertising account. For them, competition winds up being the ultimate aphrodisiac.

I hope you enjoy spending time with Samantha and Michael. As always, I'd love to hear what you think. You can contact me through my website at www.jackiebraun.com

Happy reading

Jackie Braun

MARRYING THE MANHATTAN MILLIONAIRE

BY
JACKIE BRAUN

MILLS & BOON®
Pure reading pleasure™

First published in Great Britain 2009
Harlequin Mills & Boon Limited,
Eton House, 18-24 Paradise Road, Richmond, Surrey TW9 1SR

© Jackie Braun Fridline 2009

ISBN: 978 0 263 20725 5

Set in Times Roman 10½ on 13½ pt
07-0209-40347

Printed and bound in Great Britain
by CPI Antony Rowe, Chippenham, Wiltshire

For my nieces and nephews:
Jason, Michelle, Steve, Stacey, Joanne, Jackie, Abby,
Amy, Mary, Renee, Alex, Yui, Stephanie, Eric, Nicole,
Allison, Meredith, Garrett, Roman, Payton, Sammy,
Connor, Ben, Natalie, Todd and Elizabeth.
Remarkable young people, all.

CHAPTER ONE

"AND the winner is…"

During the infinitesimal pause before the presenter read the Addy Award recipient's name, Samantha Bradford was sure her heart stopped beating.

This is it, she thought. *This is my moment.*

"Michael Lewis of the Grafton Surry Agency."

Or not.

Sam straightened in her seat, pasted a smile on her face and joined in the applause. As her palms slapped together with stinging force, her gaze narrowed on the man who was striding across the stage of the Atlanta Herriman Hotel's grand ballroom, buttoning the jacket of his superbly tailored suit as he went. She knew him well. He was admittedly handsome, sexy, smart, insightful and charismatic. He also sang off-key in the shower, preferred boxers to briefs, enjoyed watching old war movies, had the annoying habit of leaving the seat up and possessed an untouched trust fund whose worth was on par with the gross national product of some small countries.

Yes, she knew him *that* well.

Seven years earlier Samantha had been in love with him and blissfully counting down the days until she became his wife. They'd found advertising jobs in Los Angeles, put down a deposit on a town house and made all manner of grand plans for their new life together. Those plans never materialized. The reason no longer mattered as far as she was concerned, though at the time Michael had accused her of choosing her family over him. Sam saw things differently. Everything could have worked out if only the man had been capable of compromise.

They'd gone their separate ways, bitterness burning any bridge that might have remained. She'd been fine with that. Really. She'd patched up her heart, put her life back in order. Michael had moved to Los Angeles without her. Sam had stayed in Manhattan, but she too had moved on.

Then fifteen months ago he'd returned to the city and the advertising scene where she was now at the top of her game. Ever since then, all of the memories, both good and bad, that Sam had safely stored away kept threatening to tumble out. She found that damned irritating. She found the man to be even more so. Michael had taken a job with one of the city's largest ad agencies and a key rival to the one where Sam worked, which was owned by her father. She and Michael had been in competition ever since, angling for each other's clients and going head-to-head for the industry's highest accolades.

Such as the Addy.

The hands that a moment ago had engaged in polite applause balled into fists in her lap. What made tonight's loss all the more galling was the fact that just the previous month Michael had snatched up the honors she'd been nominated for in the print campaign category of the Clio Awards.

For anyone keeping score, and she knew damned well Michael was, tonight made it two and zip in his favor.

Sure enough, when he reached the podium and took the trophy in his hands, his gaze seemed to search the audience. She swore he was looking straight at her when he brought the Addy to his lips and gave it a lingering kiss. Afterward, he offered a sexy grin that had half the women in the room issuing a sigh and the other half wanting to. Sam's stomach did a familiar little flip and roll, but she reminded herself that she'd long ago conquered the weakness that would have had her falling into either category.

"Some people might say it's an honor just to be nominated for this award," Michael began. "But I'll let you in on a little secret. I really wanted to *win* this one. And victory is all the sweeter for having been chosen from a group of such talented people."

He winked in her direction.

Why you arrogant son of a...

She let the thought go unfinished. Instead, she instructed herself to take a deep breath and hold it before releasing it slowly between her teeth. She knew from past experience that the relaxation technique worked, so she tuned out the rest of Michael's short acceptance speech and continued, feeling some of her tension ebb away.

Look forward, not back.

That was her motto. The awards would be over soon. The American Advertising Federation's annual conference had wrapped up that afternoon. Tomorrow she would return to New York, and though it was a Sunday, she would be back at work. Nothing new in that. Sam spent a lot of weekends at the office. But while staying at the Atlanta Herriman she'd heard talk that the luxury chain of hotels might be looking for a new firm to handle its national campaigns. She intended for the Bradford Agency to be first in line should the rumor turn out to be true.

Thundering applause pulled her from her thoughts. Michael was leaving the stage. He held the trophy aloft in one hand as he made a fist of the other and pumped it in the air. It took an effort not to let her lip curl. She hadn't thought it possible for him to look cockier than he had on his way to receive the award. It just went to show that the man's potential in that area was limitless.

Three tables over, the people from Grafton Surry were on their feet, giving their golden boy a standing ovation. No doubt they would be toasting him with champagne late into the night. Perhaps one of the pretty, young account executives sitting at his table would offer to celebrate with him in private. Who knew? Who cared? Not Sam. Nope. She planned to go to bed early, rise before the sun and be at her desk in New York by noon. By the time Michael roused from sleep with what she hoped would be one very major hangover, she would have worked up a strategy for landing that big account.

Michael paid tribute to his win with a glass of the hotel's finest bourbon as he sat by himself in the upscale lounge that overlooked the lobby's impressive fountain. The trophy was in the center of the table, sharing space with a bowl of mixed nuts. He was pleased to have won it, especially since his success had come at Samantha's expense. Again. But victory didn't taste as sweet as he'd hoped it would. Something was missing. *Again.*

Several of his colleagues had gone to a nightclub outside the Herriman. They'd urged Michael to come along since he was the one they wanted to honor with raised glasses. He'd declined, claiming fatigue, even though he was 180 degrees the opposite of tired, which was why he was in the lounge rather than sitting alone in his room sampling something from the minibar. Wired, that's how he felt. Primed. Though for what he couldn't have said.

Until he saw her.

Sam stood framed in the lounge's arched entrance, looking like something straight out of his fantasies. But it wasn't fantasies that kept Michael awake at night. No. Memories were the culprit. Some were bitter, others sweet. All of them still beckoned him, remaining far too fresh and distracting, given the passage of time. The woman had hurt him. Now she haunted him, which, aside from the excellent job opportunity at Grafton Surry, was why he'd returned to New York. He wanted her exorcised once and for all.

Unfortunately, as he stared at her now, all he really wanted was *her*.

Sam had always had that effect on him. It wasn't until she'd essentially put her father's needs before Michael's, making her priorities painfully clear, that he'd resented her for it. He swallowed now and swore under his breath. Why did she have to be so beautiful?

Seven years hadn't changed that fact. If anything, she was lovelier now than she'd been at twenty-five. Her face had lost some of its fullness but none of its impact, dominated as it was by nearly black eyes that were topped off with a lush fringe of lashes and elegantly arched brows. Her hair was a couple of shades lighter than her eyes but just as rich, with a natural wave and sheen. She wore it shorter now. It hung to just below her shoulders, additional layers softening the appearance of her blunt chin and prominent cheekbones.

And then there was that body. Michael shifted uncomfortably in his seat as his gaze slipped south, pulled in that direction despite his best intentions. Soft curves made him want to moan. Sam had never been voluptuous, but nothing about her figure could be considered boyish. The cinnamon-colored halter-style gown she wore made it abundantly clear that every last inch of her was female. The gown dipped low enough in the front to offer a tantalizing peek of cleavage, under which a wide band of fabric highlighted the narrowness of her waist. From there, it flared out subtly at her hips. A slit up from the hem gave him a glimpse of one shapely calf. He remembered how those bare legs felt to his touch. He remembered how they felt wrapped around him.

Michael reached for his drink, finishing off the bourbon in a single gulp. Need began trickling back even before he returned the glass to the table. To counteract it, he reminded himself how ruthless she could be. Once upon a time he'd admired Sam's go-for-the-jugular approach in business. Now that they were competitors, he found it damned annoying. Last month she'd tried to sweet-talk away one of Grafton Surry's biggest clients. One of *his* biggest accounts. Only a sizable cut in his commission and long hours spent on a new campaign had kept the high-end watchmaker from jumping ship. He would be paying her back for that. Soon.

Right now he intended to call it a night. Michael raised his hand to signal the waiter for his check. Unfortunately, it was Samantha's attention he snagged. He knew the exact moment she spotted him. Her expression tightened, and for just a second he swore she looked…vulnerable. Trick of the lounge's dim lighting, he decided, and sent her a smile as he gave his Addy award a caressing stroke.

Samantha's dark gaze followed the motion and she scowled. She turned and took a step toward the exit, but then she was pivoting back and marching to his table on a pair of heels that made her legs look as if they belonged in a chorus line.

"Hello, Michael."

Her voice was as husky and provocative as he remembered. He ignored the tug of lust and in his most casual tone replied, "Hey, Sam. It's been a while."

They had seen each other a few times across crowded rooms at advertising functions, but this marked their first actual conversation since his return to town.

"Yes. It has."

"How have you been?" he asked.

"Good. Great, in fact. You?"

"The same. How's your family?"

Michael thought he'd managed to keep the sneer from his tone, but realized he wasn't successful when she replied, "I might tell you if I thought you really cared. In fact, as I recall, the last time I tried to tell you, you wouldn't even listen."

"Ancient history." He shrugged. But then couldn't resist adding, "I see you're still working for Daddy."

She crossed her arms, leaving the little beaded handbag she carried to swing from one elbow in her agitation. That wasn't what held his attention, though. The pose did sinful things to her cleavage, which in turn did sinful things to his line of thinking.

"Why wouldn't I be? The Bradford Agency is the best in town."

"*One* of the best," he corrected. "I guess I thought maybe after all these years you would have finally broken free of him."

"I don't need to break free," she objected. "I'm an account executive and a good one. I'm being primed, I might add, to take over the agency when my father retires in eight years. That means that by the time I'm forty, I'll be the one calling all the shots at Bradford. I could very well wind up in charge of my own agency before you do. I'm hardly the prisoner you assume me to be."

"Right." He nodded solemnly and ignored her jab about his foot-dragging on going into business for himself. "I forgot. You had a choice, Sam. And you made it."

They stared at each other for a long moment. He barely heard her voice above the din of conversations when she replied, "You made a choice, too."

He closed his eyes, shook his head. "Back to that already, are we?"

"What did you expect?"

"More originality on your part, I guess, given some of the advertising campaigns you've put together."

Her eyes narrowed. "I'm trying to figure out if that was intended as a compliment."

"Let me know when you decide." His smile was intentionally ambivalent.

Sam unfolded her arms. "Well, I just came over to offer my congratulations."

"That's big of you under the circumstances."

"Just say 'you're welcome,'" she said tightly.

"You're welcome." Michael angled sideways in his seat and settled one elbow over the back of the chair. Testing himself, he allowed his gaze to meander to the vee of her décolletage again. Even without her arms crossed, enough gently mounded skin was exposed to ignite his imagination and send his hormones into overdrive. "That dress looks good on you. And I do mean that as a compliment, in case you're wondering."

She shrugged dismissively. "It was just something I had hanging in my closet."

"Ah. I see you still have expensive taste." When she said nothing, Michael added, "That particular designer's fashions are very high end. I know because he's one of my clients."

"Yes. For now." She smiled sweetly and he felt a muscle begin to tick in his jaw.

"You work too hard, Sam. It makes me wonder if you're ever off the clock or if you're always scheming up ways to grab my accounts."

"I don't have to scheme for that, Michael. I just have to do my job well. As for my personal life, it's none of your business."

He shrugged. "Still, I'm surprised to see you in here.

I figured you'd be tucked in your bed by now, alarm set, bags packed and ready to head to the airport to catch the first flight to LaGuardia."

This time the muscle that ticked was in *her* jaw, making him wonder how close he'd come to the truth.

"If you must know, I was supposed to meet someone for drinks."

Michael glanced around. His amused expression belied his words when he said, "I hate to be the one to break it to you, but it looks as if you've been stood up."

"As amusing as you would find that to be, the truth is I'm the one who's late. Our meeting time was nearly an hour ago. Unfortunately, it completely slipped my mind."

"Better things to do, such as go to bed alone?"

Her eyes narrowed, making him wonder if he'd scored another hit. Then he pictured her in that bed, alone…and waiting. And he was the one who took the hit. "Sorry." Michael waved a hand. "It's none of my business."

"Right you are."

"Forget I said it."

"I've tried to forget everything you've ever said to me," she replied airily.

"Yeah?" He cocked his head to one side. "Had any success?"

"Plenty." She smiled.

"So, you're saying the past—our past—is water under the bridge?"

She nodded, looking pleased when she informed him, "That's *exactly* what I'm saying."

"Good. Glad to hear it." He reached for the chair next to his and pulled it away from the table. "Then it shouldn't be a problem for you to join me in a drink. You can drown your sorrows."

He told himself he'd only tendered the invitation to wipe that smug grin off her face. He half hoped she would refuse. His masochistic half, though, knew she would accept. Sam wasn't one to back down from a challenge or a dare. Essentially, his invitation was both. A chorus of *Halleluiah*—sung by that masochistic half—broke out in his head as she lowered herself slowly into the chair. He sought to silence it with a sip of bourbon, only to realize a little too late that his glass was empty.

Of course she noticed.

"What are *you* looking to drown, Michael?" One dark eyebrow arched as she asked the question. Before he could answer she signaled the waiter. "I tell you what. This round is on me."

Michael tapped the side of the empty glass with his index finger. He meant it when he said, "You'll get no objection. I'm only too happy to see you pay."

Sam gritted her teeth. Foolishness, that's what this was. She couldn't believe she'd let Michael trick her into having a drink with him, much less buying. She stared at the Addy award that was in the middle of the table and recalled his acceptance speech. She felt her blood pressure rise along with her anger. She should get up and leave. But that would be playing right into his hands. She'd stay. Let him be the first to call it a night. He was stuck with her company now.

When the waiter arrived, she asked for a glass of Chardonnay. Michael ordered bourbon. According to her watch, it took the server eleven minutes and forty-eight seconds to return with their beverages. She and Michael spent the time selecting nuts from the bowl and making inane comments about the conference, which was only marginally better than chatting about the weather.

"A Chardonnay for the lady and your bourbon, sir," the waiter said as he removed the glasses from his tray and set them on the table.

When he was gone, Sam asked, "What happened to Scotch?"

That had always been his drink of choice. He'd preferred it neat as opposed to on the rocks.

He shrugged. "Tastes change."

"Yes, they do." Samantha picked up her drink. "Here's to change."

"Are we drinking to any change in particular?"

She watched his fingers curl around his glass. They were long and, she recalled, exceptionally skilled. Sam chased away the memory with a sip of wine and lifted her shoulders in a negligent shrug. "I'll leave that to you to decide."

His eyebrows shot up. "I don't remember you being

so accommodating in the past, Sam. I like it. A lot." He winked then and raised his own glass. "To change."

She intended to let his remark pass without comment, even though Michael was dead wrong: he'd been the one with issues when it came to accommodation, to compromise, not her. Sam took another sip of her wine before setting the glass back on the table. Then she took a deep calming breath and offered him a bland smile. It promptly turned into a sneer. So much for biting her tongue, she thought as she launched into her attack.

"God, that's so like you to manipulate the truth. I'm not the one who issued the damned ultimatum that killed our relationship."

"No? Are you sure about that?"

"What's that supposed to mean?"

"You're the one who took a stand, Sam."

"Me? 'Come to California now or it's over.' Do those words ring a bell? If not, maybe you should go see a doctor. It appears your memory is failing." She reached over and tapped his temple where a few fine threads of silver shot through his otherwise sandy-brown hair. When had he acquired those? And why did they have to look so damned good on him?

Michael captured her fingers in his. "I postponed our wedding, moved to California without you and waited for you to come, only to have you call to say you were staying in Manhattan. So, it's your memory that could use a little improvement. Mine is just fine, sweetheart."

The endearment, issued as it was in such an insult-
ing manner, rubbed roughly across her nerves. It didn't
help that he was still holding her hand. She tugged free
of his grasp. "Don't call me that. You lost the right a
long time ago."

He made a scoffing sound. "I didn't lose it. I gave it
up gladly when you sent back my ring. Daddy—you
know, the same guy who spent your entire adolescence
kicking your self-esteem to the curb—*needed* you."

"You still don't get it." Sam shook her head in frustration and even as she called herself a fool all these
years later, she wanted him to understand. "After
Sonya's accident—"

Just as he had seven years ago, though, he blocked
her attempt to explain. "Don't. Let's not talk about your
sister or your father or anything else to do with the
past." Before she could object—and, boy, did she plan
to give him an earful—he abruptly changed the subject.
"How about another toast?"

"I can't imagine what else we have to drink to." She
meant it. After all, almost everything between them
was past tense.

Michael, of course, found the one thing that wasn't.
"How about my win tonight. You know, just to show
that you harbor no hard feelings."

He offered the same grin that he had from the podium. It was a challenge, a dare, and as such she found
herself helpless to say no.

"Why not?" she replied.

"Ah. There's a good sport."

She doubted he would think so when she'd culled half of his accounts. That was her goal. Maybe then he'd leave New York again. In the interim, she could be magnanimous and humor him. "To your win tonight."

As Sam reached for her wine, Michael had the nerve to tack on, "And the one last month. You haven't forgotten the Clio, have you?"

"No. It's fresh in my mind," she assured him, twirling the thin stem of her glass between her thumb and fingers. Half of his accounts at Grafton Surry? Why stop there? She wanted them all. "To your win, both tonight and last month." Just before taking a sip of her wine she added, "May they be your last."

His laughter came as a surprise, erupting as it did just after he managed to choke down a swallow of bourbon. She remembered that laugh. There'd been a time when she'd loved hearing it.

"I thought there were no hard feelings," he sputtered.

"None whatsoever." She nodded toward the award. "But that doesn't mean I don't plan to be the one holding that thing next year."

"It sounds as if you've got a serious case of trophy envy, Sam." He picked up the Addy and held it out to her. His tone bordered on seductive when he leaned close and whispered, "Want to touch it?"

His words awakened needs that had nothing to do with advertising or awards, and stirred up memories of quiet mornings, lazy afternoons and late nights when temptation had turned into passion and obliterated all else.

"It's heavier than it looks," he went on. "But, damn, it feels so good."

So good.

The scent of his cologne wrapped around Sam, pulling her in. Sex. She remembered what it had been like with him, how glorious it had felt. She exhaled sharply and pushed both Michael and the award away.

"Thanks, but I'll wait until I'm alone." She cleared her throat, felt her face heat at what could only be called a Freudian slip. "I mean, I'll wait until I have my own."

He studied her a moment longer than was comfortable for her. Then he shrugged and returned the trophy to the table. "Suit yourself. Of course, that might be a while. The competition in your category has gotten pretty stiff these days."

"Is that your ego talking?"

He snagged a handful of nuts. "Call it what you will. Results are what matter. And we both know what those have been lately."

"Awards aren't everything," she reminded him.

"No. They're the icing on the cake. In the end, accounts are what matter."

"The bigger, the better," she agreed, her thoughts turning to the hotel chain. If the rumor was true and she could land the account, what a feather in her cap that would be. Even her father would be impressed, and

God knew earning Randolph Bradford's approval had never been easy. If not for her sister's accident and then… Sam refused to allow the thought to be finished.

"Like Sentinel Timepieces?" Michael asked, referring to the watchmaker she'd tried to entice away.

That hadn't been what she'd had in mind, but she shrugged. "Perhaps. I go after what I want and I usually get it. Sentinel was an anomaly."

He looked slightly amused. "Is that your polite way of telling me to watch my back?" He wagged his eyebrows and added, "I'd rather watch yours."

She rolled her eyes, even as his juvenile comeback had heat curling through her belly. "Suit yourself, but don't cry foul when your preoccupation with my posterior results in a mass exodus of clients from Grafton Surry."

"Preoccupied goes a little too far. Your butt, as fondly as I remember it, isn't going to stop me from spending a little one-on-one time with the folks who are signed with Bradford."

The gloves were off, which was fine with Sam. She liked this better. Work, rivalry—they were straightforward.

"Unlike your clientele, mine is loyal, which I think you've already found out."

"I've only called a couple so far."

"Then I'll save you some time. I offer them what they want and I deliver the market. None of them is looking to switch."

"Sure about that? I can deliver the market, too." His lips curved. "And I can do an even better job of it than you."

Sam snorted. "God, you've never been short on confidence."

"Neither have you." He'd been smiling, but now he sobered. "You know, even more than your butt, I always found *that* to be an incredible turn-on."

Sam tucked some hair behind her ears and moistened her lips. Laugh in his face, she ordered herself. At the very least deliver an emasculating comeback. All she came up with was, "Me, too."

As soon as the words were out, Sam wanted to throttle herself. Why did she have to go and admit something so potentially volatile? It was bad enough to think it. After all, she'd been trying to sift out all of the softer emotions she had when it came to Michael. Here was a doozy and it was threatening to whisk her back in time.

She blamed the wine, even though more than half a glass remained. Most of all, she blamed Michael. He'd been the one to bring it up. Glancing at him now, she found a modicum of comfort in the fact that he looked as out of sorts as she felt, as if he too were wishing he could snatch back his words.

"I think I should call it a night," Sam said, reversing her earlier decision to have him leave first. "I have an early flight."

"Yeah. Same here."

With her luck they would be on the same plane, seated next to each other and then stuck on the runway during an extended delay.

After the waiter came with their check, Sam paid the bill. Michael insisted on leaving the tip, though she'd told him she had that covered, too. They argued back and forth, neither one backing down. Just like old times. In the end, the waiter wound up with one whopper of a gratuity.

They walked out of the lounge together yet not together. Sam groped for something to say as they stepped into the elevator, and the awkward silence stretched. Even when the bell dinged and the doors slid open on the tenth floor, nothing came to mind.

She chanced a glance in Michael's direction as he got out. There'd been a time when she could read every one of his expressions. She didn't recognize this one. His smile was tight as he reached for the doors to prevent them from closing.

"See you back in New York," he said, which was unlikely. They'd managed to avoid each other for more than a year.

"Sure," she nodded. "Maybe I'll bump into you at the office of one of your clients."

"Now, Sam." He tipped his head to one side and made a tsking noise. "Be good."

"Oh, I'm better than good and…" She blinked. The words were a joke, an old and very private one between the pair of them. Her rejoinder usually ended with the sensual promise: "I'll prove it to you later."

Michael's smoky gaze told her he remembered the joke, too. He leaned forward and for one brief moment she thought he was considering kissing her. A bell chimed then and the doors jolted his elbow in their effort to shut. He released them and stepped back. But the last thing Sam saw before they closed completely was Michael reaching out as if to stop them.

CHAPTER TWO

SAMANTHA overslept.

The alarm went off at the appointed time, right after which she received a wakeup call from the hotel's front desk. She ignored both and burrowed deeper under the covers, eager to go back to sleep. She could catch a later flight.

Now, as she sat in the first-class section of a 747, awaiting the departure of her noon flight, she flipped through a magazine and admitted that missing the red-eye had been no accident. She had not wanted to chance facing Michael again so soon.

She'd dreamed about him. Her face felt warm now as she recalled that in her dream, before the elevator doors closed, he'd kissed her, deeply, passionately. And he hadn't stopped there. No, he'd stepped back inside, let the doors slide closed behind him and as the lift traveled to the hotel's highest floor, he'd helped Sam off with her clothes. She'd returned the favor, every bit as eager as he. What would have happened next was obvious. But before their bodies touched, her alarm had gone off.

Sam had woken up panting and so aroused that she'd actually tried to go back to sleep and let Michael finish what he'd started. Of course, that hadn't happened. But the mere fact that she'd wanted it to, even in a dream, had her reeling. She'd been keyed up ever since, a feeling she attributed to confusion and irritation rather than sexual frustration or a flaring of old feelings. No, no. It wasn't either of those things. Closing her eyes she exhaled shakily.

"Nervous flyer?" a deep male voice inquired, jolting Sam's eyes open.

She glanced up to find Michael standing in the narrow aisle, a laptop computer slung over one shoulder and a smile turning up the corners of the mouth that had once trailed its way down her neck.

Glancing away, Sam accused, "I thought you were taking the red-eye back to the city."

"Looks like we both missed it." He dumped the laptop onto the roomy leather chair directly across the aisle from hers and shrugged out of his sports coat.

"Looks like," she managed as he arranged his belongings and took his seat.

"Actually, I turned off my alarm. When it went off, I was in the middle of a really good dream. I wanted to see how it ended."

Because she knew exactly what he meant, Sam said nothing. But as Michael fastened his seat belt, she clearly recalled helping him undo the belt on his trousers in her dream. He was a tall man, surpassing the six-foot mark by at least a couple inches. In first class, however, he was able to stretch out his legs, which he did now, looking the picture of relaxation. In contrast, Sam tensed, as if waiting for a trap to spring.

It did a moment later when he asked, "So, what did you dream about last night?"

"I have no idea. I never remember anything after I wake up," she claimed, even though that highly sensual encounter was burned into her memory.

He tipped his head sideways. "Really? Nothing? That must be a recent development. We used to lie in bed sharing our fantasies all the time."

He was dead on, but she wasn't going to go there. "Fantasies aren't the same as dreams," Sam told him matter-of-factly.

"I guess you're right, even though you can act out both." He smiled wolfishly.

She heaved an exaggerated sigh and reached for the magazine that was open on her lap. The flight to New York would be a very long one if Michael was determined to chat. Maybe if she pretended to read he would take the hint and stop talking to her.

Of course he didn't. "So, you really don't remember your dreams?" He didn't wait for her to answer, not that she planned to. He went on. "That's a shame. I *always* remember mine."

"How nice for you," she muttered with a definite lack of sincerity.

He wasn't put off. No. A sideways glance in his direction revealed he was grinning. Then rich laughter rumbled. "And I have a feeling the one from last night is going to stay with me for a long, long time."

He winked at her, once again leaving Sam with the uncomfortable yet highly erotic impression that she'd played a starring role in his dreams, too.

Thankfully, the flight attendants came through then to ready the cabin for take-off. Once the plane was in the air, Sam reclined her seat and closed her eyes, determined to nap or at least feign sleep to deter further conversation with Michael. The man was getting under her skin. It was just her bad luck that part of her wanted him there.

The captain had just announced their cruising altitude and turned off the seat belt sign when she felt Michael nudge her elbow. "Hey, Sam."

"I'm trying to sleep here," she replied, eyes still closed.

"No you're not. You're trying to ignore me."

She turned her head and allowed one eyelid to open. "Yes, but I was being polite about it."

"Right." The magazine in his hand was turned to an inside page, which he held out for her inspection. "What do you think of this?"

She opened both eyes. "The perfume?"

"No, the ad for it."

She straightened in her seat, reaching for the periodical before she could think better of it.

"The client certainly spared no expense," she said of the full-page, full-color advertisement that featured a top-name model standing in the middle of a field of flowers and holding out an ornate bottle of perfume as if making a sacrificial offering. "Is this one of yours?"

"Does this *look* like my work?" He sounded insulted.

In truth, it didn't. The composition was too stiff and staged, and the accompanying text about letting love bloom sounded sophomoric. But Sam merely shrugged. No need to feed Michael's massive ego.

"All that money to spend and this is what they came up with. Amazing." His voice dripped with such disgust that Sam had to chuckle.

"Are you jealous?"

"Hell yes, I'm jealous," he surprised her by admitting. "In addition to spreads in several national publications, this same ad is appearing on billboards and the sides of buses all over the country. And there's a corresponding television campaign under way."

She saw the dollar signs and whistled. "Someone's dining on steak."

"Want to know who?"

Curiosity piqued, she nodded.

"Stuart Baker."

The name rang a bell. "Wiseman Multimedia, right?"

"That's him. That guy can't spell innovation, much less employ it." Michael snorted.

"Yes, but look at it this way. Unlike me, Stuart Baker

will never be a threat to you in the Clio or Addy competitions. And the client obviously likes Baker's work."

"Right. Want to know what I think?" Michael asked.

"I'm waiting with bated breath," she replied dryly.

"He's got something on the person holding the purse strings at the fragrance company. You know, compromising photos or a lurid videotape."

"You have a vivid imagination. More likely, the client has more money than marketing sense."

He shrugged. "Maybe, but you have to admit, my theory is more interesting than yours."

She shrugged and put her head back and closed her eyes, figuring the conversation was over. But a moment later Michael nudged her arm again.

"If this were your client, what would you do differently?"

Sam kept her eyes closed. "I'm either trying to sleep right now or politely ignoring you. Take your pick."

"Come on, Sam. We've got some time to kill before we land in New York. Let's make the most of it. What would your ad look like?"

It was an old game, one they'd played often when they were fresh out of college and eager to tear up the advertising scene. They would analyze various campaigns, print or television, and decide what they would do to improve them. Sam had no intention of playing along now. But she made the mistake of opening her eyes and glancing at the glossy page Michael held out to her. A statuesque blonde pouted up at her. She couldn't help herself. Besides, she rationalized, talking shop with Michael was far safer than discussing dreams…or fantasies.

"Well, for one thing, I would have gone with a lesser-known model," she said.

"Why?"

"Sasha Herman has pitched everything from cow's milk to men's undershirts."

"So she resonates with the public," he countered, playing devil's advocate.

"That might be, but she also causes waves. Her increasingly radical political views aren't winning many fans among women in middle America."

"Everyone is entitled to an opinion," Michael retorted. "So Sasha is a little more vocal than most people, so what? Should she be punished for exercising her constitutional right?"

"I'm all for the First Amendment, but the fact remains that she's used her celebrity as a platform for some pretty extreme views, and it's costing her. She's fallen out of favor with a lot of Americans, including the very women who make up the client's target market." She sent him a quelling look. "No one ever said free speech was free."

"Okay. Point taken. So you'd change models and go with a less recognizable face," he said.

"Actually, I'd go with a complete unknown," Sam decided as a new ad took shape in her mind. It was black-and-white and far more sensual, fitting with the perfume's name: Beguile.

"To play up the mystery?" he asked.

"That's right." Sam nibbled her lower lip and allowed the vision to expand. "It should be a man wearing a white dress shirt, left unbuttoned to show off his incredible abs. After all, perfume is really just sex in a bottle. Women want to buy it from a good-looking man. It's part of the fantasy. If I wear this scent I'm desirable. I can entice anyone. I can *have* anyone. Even this drop-dead gorgeous stud whose eyes are saying, 'Beguile me.'"

"God, it's scary how the female mind works," Michael replied dryly.

"Oh, please," she huffed. "The female mind is no different from the male mind. We think about sex, too."

Think about it and dream about it in vivid detail, a small voice whispered.

"Go on," Michael encouraged with an engaging smile. "I'm all ears."

Uh-oh. She had wandered into boggy territory. As quickly as she could, Sam retreated. Conjuring up her most-patient and instructive voice, she replied, "Even though we're rivals, here's a key trade secret that I'm willing to share with you." She leaned toward him and whispered, "Sex sells."

"Gee. It seems to me I've heard that somewhere." He rubbed his chin thoughtfully. "Like maybe in the first advertising class I took back in college."

She lifted her shoulders. "It doesn't sound like you paid close attention."

"I did when the curvy blond junior who sat in front of me was absent. Otherwise I found her a bit too distracting, if you know what I mean."

Sam cast her gaze skyward and settled back in her seat.

"Come on. That was before we met, Sam. There's no need for you to be jealous."

"Jealous? I'm not—"

"What about the rest of the ad?" he said with a smile.

She frowned. "What do you mean?"

"What other changes would you make? I'm assuming you'd do more than switch the gender of the model."

Though she wanted to ignore him, Sam straightened in her seat and studied the ad again. It really was hideous. She tapped the bottom of the page. "Well, for sure I'd eighty-six the field of flowers."

"What's wrong with flowers? I thought women liked flowers? I send my mother a bouquet for her birthday every year. Daisies. They're her favorite. And you always liked roses. Long-stemmed red ones."

He'd surprised her with them often, she recalled now. No special occasion necessary. She'd loved getting them, loved reading the sweet notes on the cards. She still had those cards, wrapped in a ribbon and tucked away in a dresser drawer beneath her unmentionables. Somehow, they'd survived the big purge she'd done of all things Michael after their final blowup. She would burn them when she got home, she decided and concentrated on the ad.

"Women do like flowers, but that's not the point. The name of the perfume is Beguile. A patch of posies isn't a fitting image, especially since the perfume isn't even a floral scent."

"You've smelled it?"

She wrinkled her nose. "Not on purpose, believe me. One of those paper samples was tucked into last month's *Cosmopolitan*. It fell out while I was taking a quiz on…never mind."

He chuckled softly and raised gooseflesh on her arms when he said, "I remember the quizzes in that magazine. They were very eye-opening and, um, educational."

And she and Michael had a lot of fun putting into practice what they had learned from them.

Sam cleared her throat. "In case you're wondering, the perfume smells very musky and heavy."

"The kind that lingers in elevators long after the wearer is gone?" he asked.

She nearly groaned. He had to go and mention elevators and lingering. The dream was back, popping up in her mind like one of those annoying Internet ads. It chased away all thought of redesigning a perfume ad.

"Sam? You look a little flushed," he said, bringing her back to the present and making her aware that she'd been staring at him. "Are you okay?"

No, she wasn't. At the moment, she was the exact opposite of okay, and it was his fault. She handed him the magazine and settled back in her seat. "Will you be going after the account?"

His brow furrowed. "What?"

She nodded toward the magazine. "Beguile perfume. Feel free to use my ideas. I'm sure they're better than anything you can come up with on your own."

He shook his head slowly, his gaze disapproving. "That was low, Sam. Even for you."

She hated that he was right. He might try to steal another advertising executive's client, but he would never poach an idea. But at least Michael was glaring at her now rather than setting off her pulse with his sexy smile.

They passed the rest of the flight in stony silence, and when the aircraft touched down in New York they each gathered up their belongings and deplaned without exchanging so much as a word.

"So, did you win?" her mother asked.

Joy called as Sam was unpacking her suitcase that evening.

"No. I'm an also-ran once again. And you know how Dad feels about also-rans. No one remembers them," she said doing a fair impersonation of her father's resonating alto.

Joy snorted. "No one remembers them except for him. There's no pleasing that man." Which was why her mother had called it quits on her marriage the summer Sam turned thirteen.

Sam's sister Sonya, who was older than Sam by a couple of years, had chosen to live with Randolph. Sam had stayed with Joy. Even before then Randolph had been obvious in his preference for his eldest daughter, who was so like him in both coloring and temperament. Sam, as Randolph had told her often enough, was the spitting image of her mother. Even before her parents' bitter split, she'd known he hadn't meant it as a compliment.

"I hope your father was at least supportive at the awards ceremony."

"Actually, Dad left before then."

She heard her mother curse. "Figures. I'm sorry, sweetie. I know the Addy was important to you."

"Thanks, Mom." She sat on the bed next to the open suitcase and sighed. "Michael won it."

"Again? I mean—"

"It's okay. That was my reaction, too, when his name was announced. I ran into him afterward. The man is every bit as arrogant and self-righteous as he was seven years ago," she muttered.

"And as good-looking?"

"That, too," Sam admitted sourly.

"You said you saw him. Did you talk?"

"We have nothing to talk about," Sam said, before adding, "But, yes, we did have a conversation. I bought him a drink, even, to celebrate his win."

"Big of you," Joy murmured.

"I thought so. Of course, I also plan to put it on my expense report."

"Good for you." Her mother chuckled, but when she

spoke again, her tone had turned serious. "But was it all business, Sam?"

"There's nothing between us but business, unless you count bad blood." And way too much sexual attraction, she added silently.

"You know, I always liked Michael."

"Liked him? You were practically the president of his fan club, Mom. It was embarrassing."

Joy was unfazed. "He was the only young man you ever dated who wasn't scared witless of your father."

Okay, she had Sam there. "Well, he was far from perfect." The toilet seat offenses and off-key singing weren't the only things that came to mind. "Yet you thought I was making a mistake when I sent him back his ring rather than calling him again or flying out to California to work things out."

"I still think you made a mistake."

"How can you say that?" Sam all but shouted into the telephone. "You know why I did that. He wanted me to leave Sonya."

"Be fair, Sam. What he really wanted was to be sure you left your father. Michael didn't know that your sister had taken a serious turn for the worse."

"Yes, but only because he wouldn't listen when I tried to tell him. He jumped to the conclusion that I was staying in Manhattan and taking the job at Bradford to please Dad and gain his favor. Is it my fault that he got it wrong?"

"Did he?" Joy asked.

They talked about other things then, the dress Sam had worn to the awards dinner and the style she'd gone with for her hair. Hours after they hung up, though, Joy's words had memories churning.

I need you, Samantha.

Both Michael and Randolph had said so. In her father's case, though, it was the first time he'd used that exact combination of words. As Sam stalked about the quiet apartment that should have been Sonya's, she remembered the occasion quite clearly.

One month prior to her wedding to Michael and three months to the day after Sonya's car accident, he'd called Sam at the apartment she shared with Michael to ask her to meet him for lunch at Tavern on the Green. The invitation itself was unusual and should have given her an inkling that something unprecedented was about to take place. Still, the conversation that occurred in the time between their salads and their entrees had her wishing she'd followed her father's lead and ordered a vodka martini.

Randolph wanted her to stay in Manhattan and join him at the Bradford Agency. It was the first time he'd voiced any sort of objection to her moving to California. Indeed, it was the first time he'd voiced his desire to have her work with him, though she'd majored in advertising with just that intention. After earning her degree, Sonya had become an account executive at Bradford. As for Sam, even two years after graduating from New York University, her father had claimed that no account executive positions were available. He suggested she continue as an office assistant until something opened up. Michael had been the one to mop up Sam's tears and suggest not only a clean break from her father but a cross-country move.

"He doesn't appreciate you, Sam. He doesn't deserve you." Michael's words had been a balm to her wounded spirit.

So when Randolph had made his offer, Sam wanted to refuse it as too little too late. Her lips had even begun to form the words when he'd trumped every last one of her objections with his wild card.

I need you, Samantha.

There had been more to his argument than those four words, of course, as potent and ultimately persuasive as Sam found them to be. Actually, he'd laid out his case with surprising emotion for a man who rarely displayed much. He feared it would be months before Sonya was capable of returning to Bradford in any capacity. At that point she wasn't capable of independent living much less being groomed to take over the agency as he'd long intended.

Absent the heir, he'd turned to the spare.

That had been Michael's unflattering assessment when she discussed it with him later in the day. Randolph had asked Sam to take Sonya's place. Temporarily. She'd agreed. She'd already asked Michael to postpone their wedding. She wanted Sonya to be her maid of honor. Despite their father's obvious favoritism, the two had always been close.

The argument that ensued hadn't been pleasant. Recalling it now made Sam ache all over again:

Michael had been incredulous at first.

"I've given my word to my new employer that I'll start in six weeks. So have you."

They'd both landed positions at the same agency, one of the biggest and most respected in Los Angeles.

"I know. You can go ahead without me. I'll just have to hope that when I make the move, the opening will still be there."

He had run his hands through his hair. In Michael's expression she'd seen frustration, anger and, worst of all, hurt. "He's using you, just like he's used you as a glorified gopher for the past couple of years. Can't you see that?"

"He needs me," she told him.

"*I* need you, too. Don't stay, Sam."

She closed her eyes, holding back tears. Torn. That's how she felt. She still wanted, *needed* to believe that her father would someday love her as unconditionally as he did Sonya. "I can't leave right now. I'm sorry."

"You can," Michael insisted. For him, this issue had always been black-and-white. "Randolph doesn't deserve your loyalty, Sam. He won't return it."

She ignored the comment, ignored the little voice that told her Michael was right. "It's only for a little while, at most six months. The doctors say Sonya is making terrific progress."

He snorted in disgust. "And once she's as good as

new, then what? He'll have no need for you and you'll be broken up into pieces again."

"It's not like that."

Michael's voice rose. "It's *exactly* like that, and you know it."

"Sonya needs me, too."

"I like Sonya and I know it's not her fault that she's your father's favorite, but when are you going to step out of her shadow and start living your own life?" he asked. When Sam said nothing, he reminded her unnecessarily, "You're being naive if you think the job in California is going to wait six months while you work at another firm in New York."

"I know." The bigger question was, "Will you wait, Michael?"

He swallowed, looking pained. "That's unfair."

"Just answer me, please."

"Your father has made you jump through hoops your entire life for the scraps of his affection. I thought you were finally finished with that."

"This is different." It was. It had to be.

But Michael shook his head. "No, it isn't, Sam. It's just a bigger hoop with better scraps. I love you and I want to marry you more than anything in the world. But if you stay here now, I have a bad feeling that isn't going to happen."

She hurried to Michael, wrapped her arms around him and held on tightly, maybe because part of her already knew she was losing him. "Don't say that!"

He sighed and rested his forehead against hers. "Believe me. I don't want to say it. But I need to be honest."

She appreciated his honesty, but she also wanted his support. "It's just till Sonya is on her feet again and able to return to work, I promise."

She broke that promise, though not intentionally. After Sonya suffered a major setback, she called Michael in tears.

"I have bad news," she began and started to cry.

"You're staying in Manhattan, aren't you?"

"Yes. I have to. Sonya—"

"I knew it, Sam," Michael said before she could tell him about the unexpected aneurism that had burst in Sonya's brain and the doctors' subsequent grim prognosis.

"Please, listen," she cried. "You don't understand."

"I don't understand what? That you've decided our wedding isn't going to happen after all. I think I figured that out on my own."

"No. I love you, Michael. I was hoping you would come back to New York," she said. "You'll have no trouble finding a job here. We can still get married."

"Why would I move back, Sam? You've made it pretty clear where I fall on your list of priorities. You've picked trying to please your father over having a life with me."

She sank down on the bed they hadn't shared since his last trip to Manhattan more than a month earlier. Even then, things had been strained. "That isn't fair."

"Tell me about it." His tone had taken on an edge she'd never heard before. It scraped over her emotions, leaving them raw. "So, what scrap is Daddy offering you now?" he asked, alluding to their earlier conversation.

She wanted to weep, to lie back on the down comforter and cry out her heartache. She might have if pride had not come to her rescue. "I wouldn't exactly call it a scrap. He's made me an account executive at Bradford."

"Account executive, huh? It sounds like you got what you wanted."

No. What she wanted most was slipping from her grasp, but she wasn't about to grovel. Michael had made it clear where she ranked on *his* list of priorities. "Yes."

"Well, I guess there's nothing more to talk about."

"I guess not."

After she'd hung up, Sam had curled up on the bed and indulged herself in that long cry.

Now, lost in the memories from seven years earlier, she curled up on a different bed in a different apartment, surprised to discover that she still had tears to shed where Michael Lewis was concerned.

CHAPTER THREE

MICHAEL had been back in New York for more than a week, and he couldn't get Sam out of his mind. She stayed there, as pesky as a damned burr.

It was probably just as well that her nasty accusation had ended what had been an otherwise pleasant conversation. Because before then, he'd wanted to kiss her. Hell, the night prior he'd wanted to do much more than that when he'd left her in the elevator. The fact that he hadn't so much as shaken her hand was of small comfort. Ever since that night he'd been preoccupied with memories of the two of them.

She'd haunted him before, but this was ridiculous. Not to mention counterproductive. That was probably her intent, he decided. She wanted him rattled and off his game.

Seated behind his desk at Grafton Surry, Michael gave up all pretense of proofreading the copy for a print ad and gazed out the window, which boasted a respectable view of midtown. It was spring in Manhattan.

Even in this gritty, urban setting, signs of life renewing itself were obvious and abundant. As were signs of the primal urge to mate, if the pair of pigeons cooing and strutting about on his window ledge were any indication.

Maybe it was the season that had kicked his libido into high gear. Maybe it had nothing to do with Samantha Bradford at all. Or only a little, he conceded, recalling the feminine sway of her hips as she walked and the habit she had of tucking her hair behind her ears. For no reason he could put a finger on, he'd always found that habit incredibly sexy. Not to mention the sinuous way she stretched in the morning or…

He closed his eyes and bit back a groan. Damn spring. Damn hormones and urges and chemistry. And damn Sam for still having the power to mess with his mind.

"Am I interrupting something?"

Michael opened his eyes to find Russell Zelnick standing in the open doorway. Russ was an account supervisor and as such had the coveted corner office. Russ didn't like Michael. Apparently, he assumed Michael was after his job. Michael did envy Russ his larger corner office, but he wasn't after the man's position at Grafton Surry. He had no ambition to climb the ladder here. Starting his own agency was Michael's ultimate goal. It had been his goal since the day he graduated from Princeton and tossed his mortar board in the air. He was getting closer to that goal by the day, soaking up experience and knowledge, getting his name known and saving for a proper office with money he'd earned rather than inherited.

"You're not interrupting anything." Michael straightened in his seat, cleared his throat. "Is there something you needed to see me about, Russ?"

"Yes."

The other man stepped fully into the office and closed the door behind him. That was never a good sign. Nor was the fact that Russ's face was florid, his expression grim. He was breathing heavily, as if he had jogged down the hall from his office, though Michael knew Russ eschewed any kind of exercise. The man was only forty-five, but thanks to high blood pressure and the few dozen extra pounds that padded his waistline, he was a heart attack waiting to happen. His next words had Michael fearing that the big one might be coming any minute.

"I got a call a few minutes ago from John Wells at Rawley Fitness Centers. He says he wants to take Rawley in a new direction, and he feels another agency can offer him that."

The account was Michael's, one of the first he'd landed for Grafton Surry when he'd moved back from California to join their operation more than a year ago.

Michael shook his head in disbelief. "There must be some mistake. He's been happy with the current campaign. He said it was one of the best he's ever seen and very effective in reaching a wide range of demographics. We have the numbers to back that up."

"Well, someone else is offering him something better," Russ snapped.

Michael's own chest felt tight hearing that. He had a pretty good idea who that someone else was.

Russ went on. "Just what in the hell is going on here, Lewis? This makes the second account of yours in the past eight months that has wanted to bail."

"Don't worry," Michael said. "I'll call him and get this straightened out."

Russ's eyes narrowed. "Like last time? Are you saying this is just *another* misunderstanding?"

"No. More likely it's a negotiating strategy," Michael said evenly. "The economy being what it is, everyone is looking to tighten their belts."

"Yeah, well if your accounts keep looking elsewhere, belts might have to be tightened around here."

With that ominous pronouncement, Russ left. Michael wasn't worried about losing his job. If worse came to worst, he'd move up his schedule for opening the Lewis Agency. It might require him to dip into the funds he'd inherited to afford the offices he was after. Though he preferred to earn his own way, that wouldn't be the end of the world. Losing the Rawley Fitness Centers account, however, wasn't an option. Especially losing it to Sam.

He was on the phone a moment later, making his case. But after a lengthy phone conversation, the only promise he managed to secure from John Wells was for a mere half-hour appointment later in the week.

He decided it was time to pay Sam a little visit. First, however, he placed a second call. He'd already begun to play her game. Now it was time to up the ante.

Randolph never knocked before entering Sam's office. He might be her boss as well as her father, but it still bugged her that he didn't feel the need to abide by the rules of common courtesy. He burst in now as she spoke to a client on the telephone. Rather than leave when he noticed she was otherwise occupied, he stalked around the room and waited for her to wrap up the call.

The moment she did, he said, "What's the status of the Herriman account?"

Even though Randolph and a handful of other Bradford account executives had gone to the advertising conference in Atlanta, Sam was the only one who'd heard the rumors. She considered that a coup, and it helped to make up for the fact that she'd lost the Addy to Michael. Her father hadn't been pleased to learn that. Monday morning at the office had been a tense affair until she'd told him about the hotel chain's advertising concerns.

"It doesn't appear to be a rumor, although I haven't been able to get it confirmed through Herriman's advertising manager."

"I have," he shocked her by announcing.

Sam rose from her seat, not incredulous but angry and, yes, wounded. This was her account, assuming it turned out to be an account at all. And he'd gone behind her back as if he didn't trust her to do her job. "You called Sidney Dumont?"

"No, but I ran into her assistant at the gym yesterday evening. I acted as if I knew it was a done deal that they wouldn't be re-signing with their current agency, and he didn't contradict me." Randolph offered a cunning grin. "I gave him my business card and told him we would be putting together something fantastic for them to consider, and to expect a call from us in the near future."

She blinked. "Us? You mean me, right?"

Randolph smoothed down his silk tie, fussing with the diamond tack that held it in place. He liked fine things and spared no expense when it came to his wardrobe. It was only with his affection or praise of Sam that he was stingy.

"This is a big account," he began. "Herriman's advertising budget is, well, astronomical."

"I know exactly how large their budget is, Dad. I've spent the past few days researching it and their market, remember?" She folded her arms. "Are you saying you don't think I can handle it on my own?"

His smile bordered on condescending. "I think you've made tremendous strides since you stepped in for Sonya, but—"

"No!" Sam stalked from behind the desk to stand in front of him. He was a tall man, and though she had to look up to him, she didn't respect him at that moment. "I won't allow it. This is my account."

His gaze narrowed. "What do you mean, *you* won't allow it? Might I remind you who owns this agency? Might I remind you who works for whom?"

"You're not being fair to me." *Again.* She had to bite her tongue to keep from adding that. Randolph had never treated her fairly, either as an employee or as a daughter. The fact that after all these years and all of Sam's hard work he still considered the job to be Sonya's proved that.

"This is business, Sam."

"Fine." She nodded vigorously. "Then let's look at my work record. I've been an exemplary employee and you know it. I've landed some pretty major accounts for Bradford. I put in longer hours around here than anyone but you. During this past year, two of my print campaigns have finaled in the Clio and Addy competitions."

"Neither of which you won," he pointed out.

Sam lifted her chin. "That may be, but no one else at Bradford had their work in the finals."

"Awards aren't everything."

"Right you are." She went back behind her desk and with a few clicks of the mouse brought up a spreadsheet on the computer screen. "So once again I'll defer to my sales record."

"You've done well," he conceded without looking at the numbers, which no doubt he'd already committed to memory.

"So, why are you treating me as if I'm a green account executive who still needs hand holding?"

Randolph tugged on his mustache. Finally he relented with a curt nod.

"Fine. The account is yours. But I'll be following your progress closely. I don't want this one to get away."

"I'm not going to let it." Then she grinned. "Oh, and speaking of landing new accounts."

Sam told Randolph about Rawley Fitness Center's all but guaranteed defection from Grafton Surry.

"Isn't that Michael's account?"

"It *was*," she corrected.

"He's going to regret having you for an enemy." Randolph chuckled softly. "Hell hath no fury and all that."

Sam didn't care for the description. "It's not like that, Dad. Whatever was between us is long over. This is purely business."

But once she was alone she could admit that stealing her former fiancé's client offered the side benefit of being personally satisfying.

This was business but it was also a pleasure, Michael decided as the taxi cab pulled to the curb in front of the building that housed Bradford's offices in midtown. He was smiling when the receptionist took him to see Sam.

The grin slipped a notch when he stepped into her office. It was bigger than his, its view of Manhattan better since it had a higher vantage point and boasted an entire wall of windows. He found those details irksome, but since she was the boss's daughter, Michael decided not to get his ego in a knot. Nepotism had its perks.

"This is a surprise," Samantha said. She didn't rise behind her desk, which looked like a cement rectangle balanced on four metal pipes. Rather, she motioned for him to take a seat on the three-legged chair opposite it that looked about as comfortable as it did sturdy.

The decor surprised Michael. It was eclectic and far too modern for his taste. For that matter, he wouldn't have suspected it to be Sam's. They'd lived together for a time, after all. After moving into their small studio apartment in the Village, they'd picked out the furniture together, both of them gravitating toward clean lines that provided comfort.

"I'm sure it is. I thought about calling, but decided I wanted to have this conversation in person."

"Oh? Everything all right over at Grafton Surry?" She smiled sweetly after making the inquiry.

"Fine, although I had an interesting talk with the advertising manager at Rawley Fitness Centers a couple of hours ago. I believe you're familiar with John Wells."

"We've become fast friends, yes."

It took an effort not to grind his molars together when she offered a second beatific smile. "He mentioned wanting to take the advertising for Rawley in a different direction and doesn't want to renew the contract with Grafton Surry."

She made a tsking sound. "I know. Apparently he

wasn't completely satisfied with what you had to offer, though your campaign's reach is admittedly broad and well thought out. Still, when I dropped in the other day with a mock-up of my idea and some numbers I thought he might appreciate…" She shrugged. "As the saying goes, I had him at hello."

"John mentioned that he likes some of your ideas," he said slowly. That bugged Michael. Even more, it intrigued him. Just what in the hell had Sam come up with that could cost him the contract? Not to be egotistical, but he felt the Rawley campaign was one of his best.

"Stellar is what he called them when we last talked." She tucked a hunk of dark hair behind one ear and fiddled with the small silver hoop that was revealed.

Michael forced his gaze back to Sam's eyes. The amusement he saw reflected in their dark depths went a long way toward making his hormones behave. "I think I have something even better to offer him."

"Gee, Michael, isn't it a little late to bring out your A game?"

He ignored the insinuation that his other work had been below par. "John's agreed to meet with me later in the week."

He enjoyed watching her smile dissolve at the news, though he had to admit, she rallied fast. With a negligent shrug Sam replied, "A professional courtesy, I'm sure."

Michael didn't want to admit that she might be right. "I guess we'll see."

"Well, good luck." She almost sounded sincere until she added, "You're going to need it. I'm particularly proud of the new angle I came up with for the company's gyms."

She fiddled with her earring again and then tucked a handful of hair behind her other ear, leaving him with the feeling that she remembered his weakness and was doing it on purpose.

"Fitness centers," he ground out.

"Excuse me?"

"John says that calling them gyms tends to put off the female clientele. But you probably know that from all of your *research* into the company. I'm sure it was just a slip of the tongue."

It was small of him, but he enjoyed watching Sam's jaw clench.

"Is this what you rushed across town to tell me in person? That you're going to try to win back the account I snatched away with my superior campaign?"

Michael chose to ignore the superior barb. "I wouldn't say I *rushed* across town." He crossed his arms over his chest and leaned on the chair's boomerang-shaped back. "Actually, I stopped for a cup of coffee on the way. Have you tried that new place on Forty-Third Street near Fifth Avenue? They roast their own beans, you know."

"Potential client?"

"Given recent events I'm not sure I should tell you that," he said with a wry smile.

Samantha folded her hands on the desk blotter and chuckled. "Wow, Michael, you're taking this well. You're even making jokes. I thought you'd be furious to lose Rawley to me, especially given how large the account is." Her lips puckered and she whistled for effect before adding, "I probably shouldn't tell you this, but when the receptionist buzzed to say you were in the lobby, I figured you were going to be all threatening and irate."

"Would you have called security?"

"Oh, in a heartbeat." She offered a giddy smile. "And then I would have had you forcibly removed from the premises."

"Tasered, too?" he asked.

"Only if the use of a stun gun proved necessary."

"You must be disappointed, then."

The corners of her mouth turned up as she admitted, "Maybe just a little."

"Well, I prefer acting civilized…in a professional setting at least."

She sent him a quizzical look. "Is there a setting where you believe in acting like a savage?"

He hiked his eyebrows. "You don't remember?"

Sam said nothing, but the flush creeping up from her neck told him that she did remember. Vividly. Unfortunately, so did he, which was why heat of a different sort wound its way through Michael. Despite his best efforts, awareness sizzled.

"All's fair in…war and advertising," she managed after clearing her throat.

"Yes, it is."

"I'm glad that you understand that."

"Oh, I do, Sam. I do."

"It's nothing personal," she added.

But of course she was lying. *Everything* between them, past and present, was personal. His next words made that clear.

"I'm glad we agree on that, because I have an appointment with the folks at Aphrodite's Boudoir a week from Friday. I've been eyeing them for a while. After I gave them a little preview of what I have in mind for a new print campaign, they were very intrigued."

"I guess we'll see," she said blandly.

Beneath the slab of her desktop her legs were crossed. Michael nearly grinned as her foot began to swing in agitation. She wasn't as relaxed and unconcerned as she pretended to be.

"I guess we will." In a bid to turn the screws a little tighter, he added, "You must enjoy working with their advertising manager. Joanna Clarkson has been very nice to me the times we've met in person and then again today when we spoke on the phone to set up an appointment."

"She's a peach," Sam said. The foot swung faster.

"Yeah, a ripe one."

At that she planted both feet firmly on the carpet and grabbed the edge of her desk. Relaxed and unconcerned? Not in the least.

It took an effort for Sam not to shoot out of her seat.

Not only was Aphrodite's Boudoir her biggest account, the print campaign she'd put together for the high-end lingerie maker had been a finalist for the Clio. Michael knew that, of course. Just as he no doubt was hoping his references to the "very nice" and "ripe"—not to mention stunningly attractive—Joanna Clarkson would get a rise out of Sam. As if she cared. She wouldn't give him the satisfaction of losing her cool. Breathing deeply, she pried her fingers from the edge of the desk and crossed her legs.

"What? No comment?" he had the gall to ask around his smug smile.

"None. Why?" She blinked innocently. "I believe we just agreed that all's fair."

Michael nodded. "That we did."

"But you were hoping to get a rise out of me," she accused.

"I admit it. I was," he said.

"Then you must feel let down."

"As let down as you were not to have to call security," Michael agreed, but then he was shaking his head. "No, I'm more disappointed than that."

"Oh?"

"You always looked incredible when you were mad. The more ticked off you were, the lovelier and sexier you got." He appeared surprised he'd said that, but then he turned on his high-voltage smile.

Just what kind of game was he playing? Sam wondered, but found herself going along, sucked back in time. Whoever said makeup sex was the best knew what they were talking about. For a moment she was mired in memories that made her want to blush. Memories that made her burn. She plucked out a recollection that was more mundane than erotic.

"So that's why you used to leave the toilet seat up all the time? You wanted to see me turn into a raving beauty?"

He wasn't put off. "Seven years late, but you finally get it," he replied on an exaggerated wink.

"I thought you just did it to be annoying."

And, oh, how annoying she'd found it, though at weaker moments since Michael had exited her life she'd almost missed sitting on the cold ceramic of the toilet bowl. Sam drummed her fingernails on the desktop, a habit he'd once told her grated mightily on his nerves. If a blackboard had been handy, she would have scraped them down it just to cap off the experience.

Michael's expression turned brittle as he watched her hand, but then his gaze shot back to her face. "I see annoying you as a side benefit now, though not back then. I guess you could say I was blinded by love."

His tone was mocking. His flippant reference to the one-time depth of his emotions shouldn't have hurt Sam, but it did. It cut to the quick, and that left her feeling exposed as well as wounded. This time when she flattened her palms on the desktop, she pushed to her feet. It was time to show him the door while she still had a hold of her temper, not to mention her dignity.

"As entertaining as I find this short stroll down memory lane, Michael, you'll have to excuse me now. I have a lot of work to do."

He stood, as well, and with false politeness inquired, "More of my clients to woo away?"

"Oh, I've got one or two on the hook," she replied, though it wasn't quite the case…yet. The second she cleared Bradford's lobby, though, she planned to start laying the groundwork and doing the necessary research into products and markets.

"Well, don't work too hard or too late. You'll find it won't be worth it," he advised before he started for the door. Two steps from it, he stopped abruptly. Though he stood in profile to her she could tell his face had paled.

Sam followed his line of vision to the small gallery of pictures that topped the credenza on the far wall. Even before he walked over and picked up the silver-edged frame, she knew it was the one that had snagged his attention. In the photograph, Sonya was seated in a wheelchair, her head braced against its high back. Even though her blond hair was the same boyishly spiky mess it had been seven years earlier, she didn't much resemble the outgoing and energetic young woman she'd been.

It was a long moment before Michael said anything, though his throat seemed to work the entire time. Finally he asked in a quiet voice, "When…when was this taken?"

Sam walked around the desk and joined him. "This past Christmas."

"But I thought…" He glanced at her, shaking his head as if to clear it. "I thought she'd recovered."

If only that were the case. How different all of their lives and futures might be—Sonya's most of all. Sam took the photograph from his hand.

"No."

"But she was getting better. She was making excellent progress when I left for California."

He sounded baffled and no wonder, since he hadn't allowed Sam to tell him otherwise the day that she'd called. The day their relationship had suffered a fatal blow.

"She was." The head injury Sonya sustained in the car accident had affected her gross motor skills more than her cognitive abilities. With time and physical therapy she'd been expected to recover fully. "But then she suffered a brain aneurism, a residual effect of the accident, or so the doctors said. It did far worse damage than the crash."

Indeed, it had robbed Sonya of more than agility and grace. It had wiped away the last traces of her sparkling personality and keen intellect. What remained all these years later was a shell of a woman. Some things were worse than death. Every time Sam visited her beloved sister, that phrase came to mind.

"When did this happen?" he demanded.

"I think you know."

What little color had returned to Michael's face leached out again. "This is why you called to tell me you were staying in Manhattan."

"I couldn't leave, Michael. How could I pack up and go after that?"

He scrubbed a hand over his face, visibly shaken. "I didn't know, Sam. I didn't know."

"That's only because you wouldn't listen when I tried to tell you." Saying so now held none of the satisfaction she'd long thought it would, which explained why her tone was not angry but resigned.

His gaze connected with hers. Stricken, that's how he looked, along with sad, sorry and definitely shaken.

"Would it have changed anything?" she almost asked. But then she thought better of it. Maybe it was best not to know.

So instead, even though he hadn't asked, she told him. "Sonya's in a nursing facility in Bakerville. It's a little town on Long Island that's about an hour's train ride from the city."

The decision had been hard for her father to make. So hard, in fact, that Randolph had actually consulted Sam about it, one of the rare times he'd sought out her opinion on anything.

"Why not in the city?"

"Dad felt Rising Sun was the best around and that Sonya might find the small-town setting soothing. He wanted to hire a full-time nurse and keep her at home, but that was impossible since she's on a feeding tube and prone to respiratory infections."

"So, there's nothing more that can be done?" Michael asked.

A familiar sadness slipped over Sam as she considered his question. Gazing at the photograph, she used the pad of her thumb to stroke her sister's pale cheek. How Sam longed to see Sonya's face light up with her signature grin or to hear her booming laughter.

"They can keep her comfortable. They can work her muscles to ensure they don't atrophy any more than they already have."

"That's all?"

She set the photo back on the credenza. "She can't walk or talk and she doesn't appear to react voluntarily to voices or other stimuli. The doctors have been pretty clear that outside of a miracle, the way she is now is as good as it's going to get."

Michael laid a hand on her arm. "I'm sorry, Sam. *Really* sorry."

She swallowed, nodded. "I am, too." Maybe it was the sincerity in his tone that had her foolishly confessing, "Sometimes I feel very guilty for living her life. After all, the position at Bradford wouldn't be mine if this hadn't happened to Sonya."

The account executive job, as well as the uptown apartment that their father had deeded to her older sister, were both Sam's now. She'd earned them. She'd worked her fanny off for the past seven years and had the client list to prove it, even if she had yet to hear her father utter a compliment. But that didn't make the guilt ebb, especially when she looked at Sonya.

Michael's hand fell away. Sam felt it slip off her arm,

not realizing how much his touch had warmed her until it was gone. She told herself that was why she shivered when he said, "Then why don't you ask yourself why you're you still doing it?"

CHAPTER FOUR

SAM hadn't intended to make the long commute to Rising Sun Long-Term Care that evening. After Michael's unexpected visit to her office, she'd planned to work late plotting ways to reel in every last one of his clients. Work, after all, had long been her refuge, as evidenced by her appalling lack of a social life, a fact her mother pointed out at every chance.

His question nagged at her, though.

Then why don't you ask yourself why you're still doing it?

She had answers for him. Loads of them. The same answers she'd had for the past seven years when her mother posed similar questions.

As the train clacked over the tracks to Bakerville, she admitted that part of her might still be trying to earn her father's approval. That's what Joy claimed. That's certainly what Michael thought. But what child, adolescent or adult, didn't seek a parent's praise?

Besides, hearing Randolph finally say he was proud

of Sam—every bit as proud as he'd been of Sonya—wasn't the main reason she stayed on at Bradford. She'd built a career there and she was helping to build the agency that someday would be hers to run. That was why Sam worked herself to near exhaustion each week. She had an investment in her father's agency that went well beyond fulfilling an emotional need. She saw no reason to walk away from that.

She fell asleep on the train, waking with a start when it pulled into Bakerville. The nursing facility was a little over a mile from the station. Generally, Sam didn't mind the walk. In fact, she almost looked forward to it. Once one got away from the depot and small downtown area, it was all tree-lined residential streets. But today she wasn't exactly prepared for the trek. Her snug-fitting black pencil skirt and three-inch high heels were perfect for the office, but they slowed her progress on the uneven pavement.

It didn't help that it was nearly dark outside or that halfway to her destination it began to rain. By the time she reached the unassuming two-story brick building at the end of Cloverdale Lane, the light sprinkling was well on its way to a torrential downpour.

The facility sat back from the street on impeccably groomed grounds that during the day teemed with spring flowers and budding shrubs. Sam raced up the lighted walkway toward the entrance, ignoring the protest of her feet and nearly oblivious to the scent of lilacs. Inside the lobby, she took a moment to dry the rain from her face and fuss with her hair. No doubt both were a mess. Not that Sonya would notice, much less care, she thought sadly.

Technically, visiting hours ended at eight and it was ten past that now, but all of the nurses knew her and tended to look the other way. Still, she felt the need to apologize as she passed the front desk.

"Sorry that I'm a little late getting here tonight. I hope it's all right, Mae."

The heavyset blonde smiled at Sam. "No problem. Sonya's awake. In fact, she still has company."

This news came as a surprise. Sam crinkled her brow. "Company?"

Randolph had been in a managerial meeting when she'd left for the day. As for her mother, Joy wasn't likely to make the trek to Long Island by herself, especially at this time of day.

"It's a gentleman," Mae said. She leaned across the laminate countertop and in a hushed tone added, "A very good-looking one, too. Sandy-brown hair and to-die-for eyes. He had all of the second-shift nurses flipping coins to see who got to deliver your sister's evening meds."

A good-looking man? Sandy brown hair? To-die-for-eyes? A face took shape in Sam's mind. No. It couldn't be Michael. Just the same, she hurried down the corridor past the nurses' station. Her sister's room was at the end of the hall. When she was halfway to it, the door opened and Michael stepped out. He was wearing the same suit he'd had on earlier in the day, though he'd loosened the tie and undone the top button of his shirt. They both stopped, eyeing each other across the distance like a pair of Old West gunslingers waiting for high noon.

"What are you doing here?" Samantha managed at last as she continued toward him on a pair of legs that had turned to rubber.

"I…I came to…" He hooked a thumb over his shoulder in the direction of the door, but then he shook his head and let whatever words he'd been about to say drift off.

He didn't look cocky now. Rather, he appeared pale. His mouth was pinched, his gaze hollow. Grief. As Sam drew even with him, she saw it reflected clearly in the deep blue of his eyes.

"It's a bit of a shock when people who haven't been by in a while first see her," she allowed.

He gave a jerky nod. "Yes. The picture—"

"In some ways it makes her look better than she actually does," Sam finished. Maybe that was the reason she'd framed it and put it on display in her office. Sonya's office. Other than changing out the pictures on the credenza, Sam had left it exactly as her sister had decorated it.

"I'd hoped it made her look worse. I'd hoped you were—" he swallowed hard before finishing "—exaggerating."

"So you came out here to see for yourself."

"Yeah. Sorry. God, Sam, I wanted you to be wrong."

His voice was emphatic, despite being soft. Hearing it did funny things to her heart.

"I wish that were the case."

"I always liked Sonya. She had so much energy, so much imagination."

Michael referred to her in the past tense, but Sam didn't correct him. That's how they all referred to her sister when they talked about the person Sonya had been.

"She liked you, too. In fact, before the aneurism, she was pretty annoyed with me for postponing our wedding, even though she was in no shape to walk down the aisle. She thought I should have married you before letting you leave for California."

"I thought so, too, remember?"

Sam had no comeback for that. She changed the subject. "It was really nice of you to come all the way out here to see her tonight. Sonya doesn't get many visitors these days other than family. Even her closest friends only make it out a couple times a year. This is a great facility. The staff and caliber of care are outstanding, the absolute best according to my father. But its location…" She lifted her shoulders. "It's not exactly convenient."

"But you're here, and often, too, if the nurses are to be believed."

"I try to make it out a few times a week. She's my sister."

"Yeah."

Because looking at him was too hard, she focused on a spot on the wall just past his shoulder. "You know, people always expected Sonya and me to be rivals. They figured that since we were only a couple of years apart and both in advertising that we were in competition. But that was never the case. We wanted the best for each other. Sonya loved me and I loved her. I still love her."

"This must be so difficult for you." He squeezed her arm just below the elbow.

"It's harder for her."

"You know what I mean."

Yes, she did. "Some days I don't want to come," Sam admitted. "After the doctors told us she'd never recover, I just wanted to pretend that she was away somewhere. Later, God forgive me, I just wished she had died."

She didn't realize she was crying until he brushed the tears from her cheeks.

"I think that's normal, Sam. Seeing her like this is hell."

"For my parents, too." She laughed roughly. "They may not agree on anything else, but they both have been devastated by this. For the first year, my mother was sure Sonya was going to just snap out of it, like something you see in a made-for-television movie. Dad was more skeptical, but I think he wanted to believe that, too."

"And you?"

"I still want to believe it," she murmured. "Even if I know it's all but impossible."

"She wasn't very responsive when I was in there," Michael said, hooking a thumb in the direction of Sonya's room.

"She's the same way with me. Still, I have to believe she knows I come and that she looks forward to my visits...in her own way."

"I'm sure she does." They stood in awkward silence for a moment before he added, "Well, I won't keep you."

Sam nodded and stepped around him, managing to paste a bright smile on her face before she stepped through the door to her sister's room.

Michael stayed. When Sam wrapped up her visit half an hour later, he was seated on one of the sofas in the lobby. He stood as she approached. She looked exhausted, he thought, noting the slight droop to her usually squared shoulders and the dark smudges under her eyes. Despite all that, she also managed to look lovely.

"You're still here?" She sounded surprised, but was she pleased? And why, exactly, did he hope that she was?

"I decided to wait for you."

Her brows pulled together. "Why?"

Good question. Michael tucked his hands into the front pockets of his trousers and rocked back on his heels. After exhaling, he admitted, "I'm not sure."

Sam let out a weary laugh. "Well, at least you're honest."

"I was always honest."

She nodded slowly. "Yes, you were."

"Do you want a ride?" he asked.

The question had her blinking. "You drove here?"

"No, I'm offering to carry you on my back all the way to Manhattan," he replied dryly. "Of course I drove. One thing I got used to in L.A. was having a car at my disposal. I decided not to give it up when I moved back, even if I still rely on cabs and the subway at times."

She tilted her head to one side and studied him. "What kind of car do you have?"

"Why? Is that going to sway your decision?" he asked.

"No, but I am curious. You always talked about owning a Porsche."

"You've got a good memory."

"Cherry red with a stick shift," she said.

"I stand corrected. You have a *great* memory." He smiled and in a conspiratorial voice added, "You wouldn't believe the way that baby hugs the road on turns, or how fast she can go from zero to sixty on a straightaway."

Sam looked to be on the verge of grinning back at him, but then she lectured, "It's not terribly practical to own a car in New York. You must pay a fortune in insurance premiums, not to mention parking fees."

He cast his gaze skyward. "I can afford it, Sam. Remember?"

"Ah, yes. Mr. Independently Wealthy." She was one of the few women who knew Michael's net worth and was unfazed by it. Maybe that's why he'd fallen for her all those years earlier. At the moment, though, her indifference was annoying, especially when she asked, "I can't believe you dipped into your trust fund for a phallic symbol on wheels."

"It's not a phallic symbol."

"Whatever. I thought you believed in earning your own way. Isn't that why we lived in that closet of an apartment in the Village with a view of an alley rather than something uptown that offered a view of the park?"

The mention of their apartment had nostalgia beckoning before he could stop it. "The place wasn't that bad. We had a lot of good times there." He cleared his throat, snapped his mind back to the present. "As for my trust fund, I haven't dipped into it. What I spend is what I've earned."

"Self-made," she murmured.

Was she impressed? God help him, Michael wanted her to be.

"That's my plan and despite some temptation over the years, I haven't deviated."

"Right." She nodded. "No rerouting for you. Once you're set on a destination, you don't believe in taking a detour, no matter what the reason. In fact, you won't even listen to the reason."

The color rose in her cheeks. She was talking about their relationship, and they both knew it.

Michael grimaced. "We've tap-danced around this ever since I learned about Sonya, but I still haven't offered a sincere apology for what happened. If I do that now, will you accept it? Will you forgive me, Sam?"

He watched her eyes widen and her lips part. "You've waited a long time to hear me say that, haven't you?" he said.

She nodded.

"You know, you once accused me of being unable to compromise."

Her voice returned along with a wisp of humor. "Actually, I've accused you of all sorts of unflattering things over the years. That was only one of them."

"Well, you were only partly right. I would have compromised if I'd known this had happened to Sonya." He held up a hand to stop her from interrupting. "And I take full responsibility for not listening when you called to explain. I was so angry."

"I know. I was angry, too."

Since they were clearing the air, he wanted it cleared all the way. "I think you should know I still feel I was right about your father. You can't please him, Sam. Has he ever told you that he appreciates the sacrifices you've made or the hard work you do at Bradford?"

"He might not say it, but—" She shook her head. "Let's not talk about my family anymore."

"Okay."

"I'd like that ride if you're still offering." She pushed

a hand through her unruly hair. "I got caught in the rain on my walk here from the train station."

"I noticed."

He'd always liked it when Sam left her hair natural and wavy, rather than turning it sleek with a blow dryer and round brush. He reached out and wrapped one of her wayward curls around his index finger. He released it quickly, a little embarrassed to have touched her in such a familiar manner despite their personal history. Or maybe because of it.

"I look a mess." She sounded oddly self-conscious as she straightened the lapels of the soggy blouse that peeked out from the collar of her equally soggy jacket.

"I wouldn't say that." He contradicted her only to say, "More like pleasantly disheveled."

She laughed, as he'd intended. "Isn't that the same thing?"

"Maybe, but pleasantly disheveled sounds better, kind of like the difference between *used* and *preowned*. In our business, it's all about word choice. Use the right ones and even a frozen dinner can sound like haute cuisine."

Sam didn't appear convinced. In fact, she frowned at him. "I have a low-calorie grilled chicken dinner waiting for me in the freezer at home. I'm sorry, but no amount of flattery is going to make that thing more appetizing, although I'm thinking a couple of glasses of Chardonnay might do the trick."

He chuckled. "Mine is Salisbury steak smothered in

clumpy brown gravy. I was going to pair it with the nice Merlot my boss gave me for winning the Addy."

"You just had to bring that up again," she said, but her tone held humor rather than irritation. The fragile truce they'd reached appeared to be holding.

"Yeah, I did."

"Figures."

"What do you say we have dinner together?" Michael ignored the part of his brain that warned he was playing with fire. Truce or no truce, too much between them remained unsettled...and unsettling. Still he asked, "Do you know of a place around here where we can stop without having reservations?"

Sam began to laugh, delicately at first and then with unbridled humor. "God, Michael, Bakerville isn't Manhattan. I doubt any of the restaurants here require reservations. Not that it matters. They roll up the sidewalks in this town about the same time the streetlights come on."

"Oh. Then we'll head back to the city and stop someplace suitable along the way. How does that sound to you?"

"I don't know," she hedged.

"Come on. You've got to eat, and so do I. We've both admitted that we have unappetizing prospects in that regard waiting for us back at our homes. Besides, you've already accepted my offer of a ride."

"You could always drop me off at the station. The

next train leaves in about forty minutes," she said, consulting her watch.

"Is that what you want, Sam?" It was a dangerous question to ask, Michael realized, when she looked up and he found himself submerged in her dark eyes.

Wants, needs—he thought he saw them there and they had nothing to do with his Porsche. But then she blinked and whatever spell she'd cast was broken.

"What I want—would love, in fact—is a change of clothes and the opportunity to take off these damned shoes. They're proving downright lethal."

Michael tapped his chin thoughtfully. "I can't do much about the first I'm afraid, but I won't object if you lose the shoes once you're seated in my car."

"I'd just have to put them back on to go inside a restaurant."

"True, but you can kick them off again under the table." He leaned toward her, lowered his voice. "It will be our little secret."

She took a moment to answer. "Fine," Sam said at last, waving a hand. "I'm too cold, tired and hungry to argue with you."

"I don't necessarily like to win by default, but I'll take it in this instance," he said.

As they walked to his car, Michael peeled off the jacket to his suit and settled it around her shoulders. When Sam snuggled inside of it rather than handing it back, he felt another small sense of victory.

CHAPTER FIVE

THEY'D been traveling west on I-495 for half an hour, engaged in polite conversation, when Michael spied a billboard for a newly opened restaurant just off the interstate. Two exits and a few turns later, they were pulling into its parking lot in a strip mall that featured several other shops, all of which were closed for the day.

"Casablanca. Nice name for a restaurant," Sam mused as Michael nosed the Porsche into a spot under a light. "I caught part of the movie again the other night when I was flipping through channels. Humphrey Bogart and Ingrid Bergman. God, I love that movie."

Her sigh had him swallowing. "I remember."

She'd talked Michael into watching it with her once, claiming that it was, in a way, a war movie. Since he was partial to that genre, he'd agreed. It wasn't a war movie, a few Nazis notwithstanding, but he hadn't regretted snuggling under an afghan on their couch to watch it with Sam…especially given what had transpired between the pair of them by the time the credits rolled.

"Sex."

"Excuse me?" she said, and he realized he'd said the word aloud.

"Sexy," he backpedaled, as he switched off the ignition. Jingling the keys in one hand he added, "You know, the movie, the era, the characters."

"Oh." She didn't look convinced.

Hoping to take the focus off his Freudian gaffe, he pointed toward the restaurant. "I'm guessing the food here won't be quite as sophisticated as the film that inspired the place's name, but it's bound to have our frozen dinners beat all to hell."

"True enough." Sam slipped her shoes back on and then flipped down the passenger-side sun visor, exposing the lighted mirror on its back. As she pulled an assortment of compacts and tubes from her handbag, she said, "This will just take me a minute."

He shrugged. "No hurry."

Although Michael tried not to, he couldn't help sneaking a peek as she applied lipstick, freshened up her blush and eyeliner, and then attempted to tame her wild hair with a little finger combing. Sam was a no-frills sort of female in so many other ways. Maybe that was why he'd always found watching her primp to be such a damned turn-on.

Uh-oh. We're not going there, he warned his already wayward libido. He got out of the car, taking refuge in the cool evening air. When she joined him a moment later, he'd managed to shift his hormones back into neutral, but he had the sinking feeling they wouldn't be staying there.

Given the hour, the dinner crowd had thinned considerably, so he and Sam were seated immediately. The place was hardly on par with the restaurants back in the city where Michael regularly dined, but the atmosphere was pleasant, the staff friendly and efficient and, well, he couldn't fault the company.

Warm Italian bread and the wine they ordered arrived while they looked over the menu.

"Are you still crazy for pasta?" he asked. "The fettuccine with asparagus and roasted red peppers sounds pretty good."

"Ooh, it does. But I was thinking about something I could really sink my teeth into, like a nice medium-rare steak that's just dripping in juice." She made a moaning noise that had his interest shifting away from the menu's selections. "I haven't had something like that in a long, long time."

"I know exactly what you mean," he mumbled.

Though he'd hardly lived as a monk since their split, Michael hadn't enjoyed a truly satisfying sexual encounter with a woman since Sam. That was galling to admit even to himself. She glanced over at Michael now and smiled. Though it was clear from her open expression that she had no idea the direction his thoughts had taken, he felt the blood begin to drain away from his head. He stanched the flow by looking away and reaching for his wineglass. Asking the woman to dine with him was proving to be the kind of challenge that made Odysseus's trials look like a walk in the park.

He took a liberal sip of Chianti. "Why don't we order both entrees?"

Her gaze connected with his. "And share?"

"Sure."

She seemed surprised by his suggestion, though they'd always done that in the past. As a couple. Of course, they weren't a couple now. They were...

"I guess we could do that," she said slowly. "As long as I get to choose the dressing for the salad that comes with the steak."

Sam had always been good at bargaining.

"Can I put in a request for the house Italian?" he asked.

"You can." She'd always been good at getting her way, he recalled when she added with a smile, "That doesn't mean I'll order it."

No, they weren't a couple. At this time, Michael wouldn't consider them to be friends, although it was possible they were heading in that direction. He wasn't sure friendship was what he wanted or even in his best interests. What he did know was that they were rivals. They were a pair of driven and determined competitors. Adversaries, if John Wells's defection was any proof. Even so, Michael was smiling right back at her when he set his menu aside.

* * *

They had finished their meal and passed on dessert. Though the hour had grown late and only a couple other tables in the quaint eatery were occupied, they lingered, talking about everything but advertising accounts and steering clear of any mention of Sam's father.

After finishing his initial glass of wine, Michael had switched to coffee, not only because he was driving but because he'd decided it was best to keep a clear head around Sam. Without anger, misguided though it had turned out to be, to act as a stopper, old feelings and desires kept bubbling to the surface. He was now on his third cup. He blamed caffeine for the fact that his pulse was racing, though part of him suspected the woman across from him was partly to blame. He'd forgotten how alluring, how downright intoxicating, her company could be.

Sam also had switched from wine after a single glass. Now, she was sipping tea, some herbal variety that she claimed was rich in antioxidants. She smiled at him, further revving his pulse. "You know, Michael, I'd forgotten what a good conversationalist you are."

"Conversationalist," he repeated, slightly annoyed. It wasn't exactly what a man wanted to be known for.

"Do you still subscribe to three different newspapers and half a dozen magazines?" She laughed then, the sound taking him back in time right along with her words. "God, our recycling bin was always overflowing."

"I've cut back on traditional subscriptions," he

replied. "I read a lot of publications online these days. It's more convenient, given my schedule, and fewer trees have to die so I can remain informed."

She rested her chin on her linked hands, looking suitably impressed. "Are you an activist now, too?"

"I wouldn't go that far, but I try to do my part for the environment where I can." Since she'd been the one to insist on recycling, he added, "See, Sam, it turns out you were a good influence on me."

"Not good enough if you're driving a car in Manhattan where public transportation is not only abundant but relatively cheap and convenient."

He drained the last of his coffee and set the cup back on its white saucer. "Tell me you don't like my car," he challenged.

"I don't like your car." But she glanced down at her teacup after making the statement.

"You are such a liar. I saw you stroke the leather seat when you thought I wasn't looking. You all but purred." And he'd nearly moaned.

"I don't like your car," she stated a second time. This time she maintained eye contact, but a grin lurked around the corners of her mouth. Then her laughter, as rich and inviting as he remembered, erupted. "I love it, okay? I absolutely *love* your car." She leaned back in her chair, folded her arms. "There. Are you happy?"

"Ecstatic. I knew you did. I could always read you like a book, Sam. And you haven't changed a bit."

She straightened, mirth vanishing as quickly as it had

come and he was sorry to see it go. "I have, Michael. I've changed a lot."

"I didn't mean it as an insult. Honest. Why are you taking it as one?"

"Because I don't want you to think that I've been stuck in some sort of time warp since we parted ways seven years ago. I might still be working for my father, Michael, but I'm a different person these days."

He nodded slowly. He could see it for himself, though he still found her ties to Randolph troubling. After all, Sam may have changed, but he doubted her father had. The bigger worry for Michael, though, was that he found this new Sam to be just as interesting and, if possible, even more appealing than the old one. How did that fit into his present plans? How was he supposed to move on with his life and purge all remnants of her from his consciousness if he started falling under her spell once again?

As much for her benefit as for his, he said, "We're both different, Sam."

"I suppose so. Experience and maturity have a way of changing people."

Her words offered a way to lighten the mood, and Michael decided to take it. "Is that a polite way of saying that you think I was immature before?"

"I don't think I should answer that question while we're in the midst of an otherwise pleasant evening."

"It has been a pleasant evening," he said.

"Surprisingly so," she replied, sounding amazed.

He ran his tongue over his teeth. "There's no need to pull out the sledgehammer. The point has been made."

Sam laughed, as she was sure was his intention. He'd always been able to take a potentially volatile situation and add just enough humor to keep it from exploding. She opted to follow his lead.

"In advertising jargon, I guess we're what they call new and improved."

He chuckled. "Yeah."

Though they'd shied away from discussing work, she figured this was a safe topic, and so she added, "I've always wondered who coined that phrase and how it managed to catch on. I mean, how can something that's new also be improved? It's either one or the other. It can't be both."

"I don't know," he surprised her by saying. "I like to think of myself as both."

She sipped her tea to keep from asking the obvious questions his rejoinder raised. Of course, that didn't stop her from thinking them. How was Michael new? How had he improved? As Sam began considering possibilities to the latter question, a sound vibrated from the back of her throat.

All hope that Michael hadn't heard it evaporated when his brows rose. Even in the dim light of the restaurant, she saw speculation and something a little more potent infuse his gaze. "Is that a good *hmm?*" he asked.

"A sigh is just a sigh, as the song goes and sometimes a *hmm* is just a *hmm*," she told him.

"Ah." He nodded. "That's a clever reply given where we're eating."

"I thought so."

Their waiter arrived then. "Can I get either of you anything else?"

Michael glanced at Sam, who shook her head, and so he told the young man, "No, we're all set. You can bring the check any time."

After the waiter withdrew, Sam reached for her handbag. "Let me pick up the bill. It's the least I can do to thank you for the ride back to the city."

"Not this time, Sam. Besides, technically, it's my turn to buy." When she frowned, he added. "You paid in Atlanta. Remember?"

She nodded. She remembered. Indeed, her memory was in overdrive at the moment. She was recalling all sorts of things. "You were a pretty cheap date on that occasion."

He sent her a cocky grin. "I won't be the next time."

The next time?

I should correct him, Sam thought. They may have reached a fragile truce and settled a painful misunderstanding from their past, but they wouldn't be sitting down to dine or drink together again anytime soon. She *was* a different person than she'd been seven years ago. Despite that, she couldn't risk her heart again. She also had her career to think about, and at the moment it put her and Michael squarely at odds.

She opened her mouth to tell him this evening would be the end of it. There would be no next time. But the words that came out were, "Fair enough."

As they walked through the parking lot, Michael surprised Sam by handing her the keys.

"What are you doing?"

"Letting you drive." His smile was slow and knowing and all the sexier for it. "You know you want to."

She merely shrugged. But, oh, how she did. It had been years since she'd been behind the wheel of a car with an automatic transmission, let alone a finely honed sports coupe with a stick, but that didn't stop her from being eager to put the Porsche through its paces.

Sam gave him high marks for patience and restraint as gears ground and the clutch popped during her first few attempts to go from first to second.

Glancing sideways, she offered, "Sorry."

"Don't apologize. You're doing well," he told her. "You're almost a pro."

"Right." She snorted out a laugh. Now she knew for sure he was just being polite. "I'll understand if you want to rescind the offer to let me drive."

"No. Keep going. I'll help." He laid his hand over hers on the stick, applying subtle pressure when it was time to shift. Even after she'd merged the Porsche onto the highway and shifting was no longer necessary, Sam left her hand on the stick and Michael's fingers remained loosely threaded through hers.

They were back in Manhattan before she was ready to be. Once there Sam turned the driving back over to Michael. Though the hour was late, the traffic remained far too heavy for her comfort, and the lights required too much shifting.

Her apartment was on the Upper West Side. It wasn't large, but it did have an outdoor space, something rare in its price range. At one time the apartment had belonged to her paternal grandparents, who'd bequeathed it to Randolph. He'd deeded it to Sonya upon her graduation from college. When Sam matriculated from New York University a couple of years later, she'd received an all-expenses-paid trip to Hawaii. As gifts went, it was generous, but it paled in comparison to what her father had given his eldest daughter. Everyone knew it. Sonya, hoping to keep the peace at the time, had asked Sam to come live with her in the apartment rent free. Pride had forced Sam to decline. She'd swallowed that same pride, she realized now, when two years later she'd moved into it alone.

As Michael circled the block for the fourth time, looking for a parking space that was within reasonable distance of her building, Sam said, "You don't need to walk me to my door, you know."

"Right. I'll just drop you at the curb, or better yet, slow down and have you jump out." He made a scoffing sound. "Please. My mom would have my hide."

At the mention of his mother, Sam smiled. If there was one thing Sam envied Michael, it was the relationship he had with both of his parents. Drew and Carolyn Lewis were kind, generous to a fault and loving. She and Michael had spent lots of time in their company, not out of a sense of duty as she'd often felt when visiting with her father, but because they'd genuinely enjoyed being with them.

"How is Carolyn?" she asked.

"As active and outspoken as ever." He snorted out a laugh. "I think my dad's a little worried that a few of the women in her Friends of the Arts committee are going to pool their money and put out a hit on her."

Sam chuckled. Carolyn, much like her son, preferred things done a certain way. *Her* way. It helped to smooth most ruffled feathers that her way often made the most sense.

"She must be happy to have you back in New York."

"Yeah." Even in profile his smile was easy to read. "She is. Dad, too. He and I try to meet at his club once a week for a game of squash."

"Is he still beating you?"

"Only every single time," Michael admitted with a wry chuckle. "The guy may be in his late sixties and retired but he hasn't slowed down at all."

"Maybe you're the one who's slowing down," she teased. "All those caterers' spreads at photo and commercial shoots. They start to take their toll."

He grunted. "Please. I'm the same weight I was when I graduated college. Dad only beats me because he has more free time to polish his game."

"What a spin, Lewis. Maybe you should forget advertising and go into politics," she said.

"Well, that's my story and I'm sticking to it."

He sent her a wink that shouldn't have had her pulse revving, but it did. Sam concentrated on the purr of the Porsche's engine instead. On the fifth time around the block he finally spied an open space. Michael sped up to beat a more humble subcompact to the spot, wedging the sports coupe into place with a minimum of jockeying.

After coming around to open Sam's door, he warned, "No lecture on how impractical it is to drive an automobile in the city."

"You may not believe this, but I wasn't planning to offer one." She patted the dashboard before rising. "After getting behind the wheel of this bad boy, I understand perfectly your decision to keep a car."

He acted startled. "My God. That guy I passed in Times Square last week was right. It *is* the end times."

"Very funny. Let's just say I'm a little more forgiving of your participation in the destruction of the Earth's ozone layer. This car's like an addiction. You can't help yourself."

"Isn't that the truth?" he murmured.

Sam swore he leaned closer as he said it, his gaze turning molten before dipping to her mouth. But then he pressed a button on the key fob, causing the car to chirp. It was secured. She felt vulnerable as he placed his hand on the small of her back and nudged her in the direction of her building.

Sam didn't say a word until they arrived. After nodding a greeting to her doorman as they crossed to the elevator, she told Michael, "Thank you again for tonight."

"You're welcome." The elevator arrived and they got inside. As the doors closed, he added, "I can honestly say I didn't think I would be buying you dinner after learning about the Rawley Fitness Centers account this morning."

"We agreed that wasn't personal, just a hazard of our business." Sam knew it was more than that, though. For the first time, she had regrets, not about her attempt to win over one of his accounts, but about her motives for doing so.

"Business. Right." He waited for her to press her floor number. As the elevator began its ascent, he said, "It looks like we're going to keep getting in each other's way, Sam."

"I don't think so. Manhattan's a large enough city."

"That's not what I mean and you know it." He stepped closer and in a seductive whisper said, "We're both after the same thing."

"The Rawley Fitness Centers account?" she inquired.

He waved a hand in dismissal. "That's a symptom, not the actual condition."

"What are you saying? That we're sick?" She wanted to laugh, but it came out sounding more like a moan. She was feeling a bit peaked right now.

"Yeah. And it's incurable," he confirmed. "We both want to be the best."

The elevator reached her floor and the doors parted, which was a good thing since the space inside the car had gotten much too confining for her comfort. Her apartment was the third door down. Needing to have something to do with her hands, she pulled out the key as they walked.

"Well, thank you, Dr. Lewis, for that eye-opening diagnosis. I didn't realize being competitive was a disease."

"It is. A contagious one, too."

"I'm sorry," she said in her most sincere voice.

He appeared baffled. "For what?"

"For giving this disease to you. We both know it wasn't the other way around."

She figured he'd argue. In fact, she almost hoped that he would. But he merely shrugged. "Who gave it to whom doesn't matter now. We've both got it." He leaned close enough for his breath to tickle her ear when he whispered, "Bad."

"W-well, here we are," Sam stammered. "This is my door." Having said so, she still checked the number to be sure. Then she slipped the key into the lock and turned it. Conjuring up a polite smile, she told Michael, "I guess this is where I say good-night."

"I guess it is."

"Good night."

"Good night, Sam." But he didn't turn to leave. He

leaned against the wall just outside her apartment, looking entirely too sexy. And that was before he inquired, "So, what happens in the morning?"

"What do you mean?"

"Will you resume targeting my accounts?"

Oh. That. She hadn't decided.

"I can't very well back away from the ones I've already contacted," she admitted in all honesty. Although she would have to closely examine her motives. So she told him, "If I think I can offer any of your clients a superior campaign, I'll go after them."

"Fair enough." He nodded. "You can expect the same from me."

"All right." When he continued to regard her in that intense way of his, she opened the door and stepped inside her apartment. Facing him, she said, "Maybe it isn't such a good idea for you to fraternize with the enemy."

Far more than the threshold was between them and they both knew it. Yet, despite the day's revelations, an invitation hovered on Sam's lips. Though the hour was late, she didn't want the evening to end, which was why she decided to close the door.

Michael knocked almost immediately, a fact that had her grinning. So, she wasn't the only one who wasn't eager to part. Excitement bubbled, a good portion of it sexual. She reminded herself to play it cool. Pasting a bored expression on her face, she pulled open the door. Blinking at him, she said, "Yes?"

"I take issue with that fraternizing comment."

"What?" She cleared her throat. The bubbles of a moment ago popped unceremoniously, forcing her to quickly realign her thoughts. "It's just a figure of speech, for heaven's sake."

Michael shook his head. "It's inaccurate, Sam. And I want to be sure you're clear on this. *Nothing* that has occurred up until this point can be considered fraternizing with the enemy."

Well, that was blunt, not to mention humbling. It was her ego that popped this time. And to think she hadn't wanted the night to end. Now she couldn't wait to close the door and have it be over.

"Look, Michael, I—"

The rest of her reply never made it past her lips. He cut it off when he framed her face with his hands and leaned in to cover her mouth with his. Michael didn't step into her apartment, but he'd breached a boundary just the same. And Sam allowed it. Allowed it? Hell, she contributed to it, kissing him back every bit as enthusiastically. The encounter was infused with all of the passion and promise she remembered so vividly, though she'd done everything in her power during the past seven years to forget it. And it ended far too quickly for her liking. Even so, they were both breathing hard and heavily when he pulled away. They stared at each other in stunned silence.

"Wow." Sam murmured the only word that sprang to mind and, in truth, she felt lucky to be able to verbalize anything intelligible.

"Exactly." Though Michael appeared to be just as dazed as she was, he also looked pleased.

He touched her lips with the tip of one finger and then backed away. Just before turning to leave, he said, "Now *that's* what's called fraternizing with the enemy."

CHAPTER SIX

IN THE days that followed, Michael considered calling Sam. For that matter, immediately after the kiss he'd wanted to finish what he'd started. Sam hadn't appeared eager for it to end, either. But he'd nixed that idea, and for the better part of a week, he'd managed to resist the urge to dial her office number.

What would he say to her? "Hey, Sam. I was wondering if you'd like to *fraternize* again."

That wasn't a good idea, for too many reasons to count. One of those reasons, however, ultimately prompted him to call her. She picked up after the first ring.

"This is Samantha Bradford," she offered in a no-nonsense tone that still somehow managed to turn him on.

He pictured her wearing something professional as she sat behind that ugly industrial-looking desk and tucked a handful of dark hair behind one of her ears. In the image that his mind conjured up, a flirty little gemstone winked at him from the exposed lobe. It was all he could do not to groan.

"Hi, Sam. It's Michael. I'm calling to offer my congratulations."

There was a pause, then, "Are you referring to the Rawley Fitness Centers account?"

"You haven't gotten any of my other clients to sign on the dotted line, have you?"

Her laughter trilled. "Not yet. These things take time, Michael. So, you spoke with John Wells?"

"A few minutes ago, yes. He said that while the work Grafton Surry has done for Rawley Fitness Centers has been top-notch—and that's a direct quote, by the way—they've decided to go in a different creative direction and won't be renewing their contract with us."

"For some reason I almost want to apologize," she surprised him by saying.

Where a week ago Michael had been angry enough to punch out a wall over the Rawley account, today he was feeling more philosophical.

"Don't. It's the nature of the business. Besides, it frees up some of my time to go after a new client or two, hopefully with even deeper pockets."

That was his plan. Just the day before, his father had shared some promising news with Michael—right after annihilating him in their weekly squash game.

After Michael had mopped the perspiration from his face and demanded a rematch, Drew had said, "Sorry. I don't have time to beat you again. Your mother and I are meeting friends for dinner. But I heard something that might make losing to me for the fourth straight week less painful. Our gardener has a cousin who works as concierge in the Manhattan Herriman. Apparently vacancies are up at Herriman hotels in several key American markets, including New York. Management is looking to change that, starting with an improved multimedia advertising campaign. Whatever agency they have now is out."

Michael wanted to ensure that Grafton Surry was in.

On the other end of the phone line, Sam said, "Clients with deeper pockets. Do these clients have names?"

He may have lost the Rawley account, but his competitive spirit hadn't died. "Like I'd tell you."

She laughed. "I had to try."

Yes, she did. Sam had always been relentless in pursuing what she was after. Some men might have been put off by that. Michael had considered it an attractive quality since it mirrored his own determination. Indeed, the only time he'd found it tedious was when she'd applied it to gaining her father's notice. In that case, he'd wished she would finally accept defeat and move on.

He brushed that counterproductive thought aside and asked, "What do you say I treat you to dinner to show you there are no hard feelings?"

"Dinner?"

"Yeah." When she still said nothing, he added, "It's the last meal of the day, generally eaten late in the afternoon or early in the evening."

"Funny. You want to treat me? I thought it was my turn to buy," she reminded him.

"Does that mean you'll have dinner with me, then?"

"I probably shouldn't, but I suppose now that you've clarified your definition of what constitutes fraternization it won't hurt."

Michael cleared his throat. "About that, Sam. I'm wondering if I should apologize."

"For what?"

"For the kiss," he replied.

"Gee, Michael, it wasn't *that* bad."

His laughter rumbled out even as his ego deflated. "Oh, I can do better. Much better. As you well know. So are we on for tonight?" Then, to clarify, he added, "For dinner, not the other."

"Oh, sorry. I'm not free tonight." She waited a beat. "For either, but especially not the other."

"I see." God help him, he did. In his mind Michael pictured Sam looking as lovely as ever and out on the town with someone else. Someone male. Someone male who had his hands on her hips and his lips cruising down her naked…

Thankfully the image popped when she said, "I'm going to see Sonya after work."

He expelled a breath but didn't think twice before asking, "Do you want some company?"

Sam was clearly surprised. "You're offering to come with me? You want to see her again?"

"I am and I do." Even though it hurt like hell to see

Sonya the way she was, he did want to see her. Like Sam, he wanted to believe that in some way she knew Michael was there, sitting by her bedside, filling in both sides of the conversation and stroking her hand. What's more, he didn't want Sam to have to go alone. "I can drive. Or if you'd prefer, you can get behind the wheel."

"Does that mean we'll be eating at Casablanca again?" she asked.

"Only if that's what you want."

She made a sexy humming noise that had his mouth going dry. "Not tonight. Why don't we grab a bite before we head out of the city? I'm in the mood for Thai food. Are you game?"

"Yeah, but what about visiting hours? Won't we be cutting it close if we have dinner first?"

"That's all right. The nurses are pretty flexible when it comes to family. As long as I leave by nine-thirty, they don't care what time I get there."

"Okay. So, Thai food it is. I know this great place," he began at the same time Sam said, "I've been wanting to try…"

"Sorry. You were saying?" Michael asked.

"There's a relatively new restaurant that I've wanted to try, but not many of my friends are fans of Thai food." And she'd remembered that Michael was. "But we can go to the place you were mentioning. Where is it?"

"A couple blocks from the Guggenheim Museum on Fifth Avenue."

Her laughter rippled. "That's the one I'm talking about. Sounds like we're on the same wavelength."

That had happened a lot back when they were a couple, he recalled. They'd finished each other's sentences. He'd sworn sometimes she'd been privy to his thoughts and he to hers, which made it all the more ironic and painful that a lack of communication had contributed to their breakup.

"What time should I pick you up and where? Your office? Or do you need to swing by your apartment first?" he asked.

"How about we meet at the restaurant at five-thirty? I'll call and make reservations."

"Afraid to let Randolph to see you…fraternizing?" Michael decided to let her decide in what way he meant the word this time.

Sam bypassed his innuendo completely. "Actually, I'm doing this for the benefit of the environment. You'll be driving out of your way to come pick me up here."

Michael didn't buy her excuse, but he let it go. He was in no hurry to see the man who at one time was to become his father-in-law.

"See you at five-thirty."

Sam had switched off her computer and was pulling on her jacket, happy to call it a day, when Randolph walked into her office.

Without so much as a greeting he said, "Catch me up on the status of the Herriman account."

Sam glanced at her watch. She would be pushing it to make it to the restaurant on time, especially if she couldn't get a taxi right away. "Can this wait until tomorrow, Dad? I've got someplace to be."

"Are you going to see Sonya?"

"Yes," she answered. Then, because she wasn't one to lie, even by omission, Sam added, "And before that I'm having dinner. With Michael."

"Michael Lewis." Randolph spat out the name as if it were poison. "When did this happen?"

She tucked some files into her attaché case and feigned confusion. "When did what happen?"

"You know exactly what I'm referring to. Good God, Sam!" he exploded. "I can't believe you're seeing him again."

"I'm not *seeing* Michael. Exactly. We're just…" The kiss made it impossible to finish the sentence with friends. Friends didn't kiss the way she and Michael had the other night. Nor did they respond to such kisses with feverish abandon.

"Can't you see what he's up to here? You've taken away one of his clients, nearly two when you think about the deal that fell through with the watchmaker. Mark my words. He's after something."

"Like what, my accounts?" She laughed. "Sure he is. There's nothing unethical about competition."

This didn't sit well with Randolph. "Tell me you haven't shared news about Herriman with him."

"Please. I'm not stupid. Of course, neither is Michael.

I wouldn't doubt he's heard the news. For that matter, I wouldn't doubt that half a dozen other Manhattan ad executives are angling for it as we speak." She sent her father a flinty stare. "But I have no intention of letting that account go to anyone but Bradford."

Her father nodded, but he didn't look reassured. "Heed my advice and watch your back, Sam. Don't trust him."

She exhaled in annoyance. She and Michael weren't back together, but she still felt pitted between the two men. "You make it sound as if he's out for revenge or something."

"Maybe he is. You didn't part on the best of terms."

"That was seven years ago." Yet it felt like yesterday. But for her father's benefit Sam asked, "What's he going to do to get revenge, Dad? Try to break my heart?"

Randolph folded his arms over his chest. "He did that once, as I recall."

"Only because I let him."

"Sam—"

He was winding up for a lecture, she could tell. Even if she'd had the time, Sam didn't want to hear it. "We're not back together." That much was true. Whatever they were, she and Michael weren't a couple. "He's taking me out to dinner as a goodwill gesture, more or less. He wants to show me there are no hard feelings over the Rawley account."

Randolph's harsh laughter echoed in the room. "Sure

he is. And you buy that? If so, maybe you're not the right person to run Bradford when I retire after all."

Sam blinked. She wanted to believe that her father had only said that to make a point. She needed to know with certainty that after the seven years she'd all but slaved at his knee that he couldn't possibly consider leaving her out in the cold. But a lifetime of falling short in his eyes made it impossible to muster the conviction required to chase away all doubt.

On the cab ride to the restaurant, she mulled over Randolph's words. She arrived fifteen minutes late thanks to an accident that had further snarled rush-hour traffic.

As soon as she saw Michael, the conversation with her father was forgotten. Everything was forgotten except the lovely, albeit dangerous, effect the man had on her pulse.

"Sorry I'm late," she said as he rose to his feet to greet her.

"No problem." Then he smiled and asked, "Mind if I satisfy my curiosity?"

The unexpected question threw her, but only for a moment. "I guess not, as long as it doesn't involve lewd and lascivious conduct. I hear that the law frowns on that."

"Spoilsports." He reached out to tuck some hair behind her ear and frowned. "Hmm. Little silver hoops. I was picturing gemstones."

She blinked at him. "You were? When?"

"When I talked to you on the telephone earlier."

His response had heat zipping through her. Before Sam could think better of it she asked, "What else were you picturing?"

Michael shook his head. "I'd better not say. I think that might fall under the heading of lewd and lascivious."

She laughed even as she fought the urge to fan herself. "You know, I always found your obsession with my earrings to be a little weird."

"It wasn't just your earrings. It was your ears, too. And, as I recall, you liked it when I did this." He leaned over and expelled a soft breath that caused her to shiver.

Given her reaction, Sam figured there was no point in denying his claim. Instead, she said, "Why don't we take our seats?"

Once again it was late when they returned to the city from visiting Sonya. Once again Michael insisted on walking Sam to the door of her apartment. And once again he kissed her until they were both breathless and feeling needy.

"This is quickly becoming a habit." He shoved the hair back from his forehead.

"I was thinking the same thing."

"Yeah?" One brow shot up. "Have you determined whether it's a good habit or the kind that needs to be kicked and quick?"

"Not yet."

"Me neither." He exhaled sharply. "I'd better go."

Sam wanted him to stay. In fact, an invitation hovered on her lips. They could uncork the bottle of wine that was chilling in her refrigerator and...talk. Clamping her mouth shut, she nodded in agreement with him.

Michael had been sure she'd been about to ask him to come in. He wasn't sure whether he felt relieved or disappointed that she decided against that. Nor was he sure why he told her, "I'll be out of town for the next few days on a commercial shoot in Big Sur, but I'll have my cell if you need to reach me."

"Big Sur, hmm?" she said. He pictured her there, wearing a skimpy bikini and frolicking in the surf. The image popped like an overinflated balloon when she added, "Remind me to go after that account next."

"Very funny."

She grinned. "Have a safe trip. I'll see you when you get back."

Even though she offered the words casually, Michael's heart gave a curious thump.

Michael was happy to return to New York even though the weather in California had been gorgeous and the trip productive in more ways than one. After wrapping up the photo shoot, he'd spent a night in the Beverley Hills Herriman. He'd toured some of the newly renovated rooms and then sat poolside with other guests, subtly gathering their thoughts on the services and amenities that were available either for an extra fee or gratis.

Afterward, ideas began bubbling, percolating intensely for a flashy multimedia campaign that he felt certain would deliver the numbers Herriman's people were seeking. He'd spent the nonstop flight home working on it and then headed straight to his office to go over his ideas with the art department and run some more numbers. He didn't arrive home until after eleven, too late to call Sam, even though with her equally crazy schedule, there was a good chance she was up. He just wanted to hear her voice.

Not sure how he felt about that, he decided against calling her the following day, too.

In the end it didn't matter. They literally bumped into each other late that morning in the lobby of a midtown office building.

"Of all the lobbies in all the buildings in Manhattan, you had to walk into this one," Michael said, borrowing and doctoring a line from *Casablanca*.

Sam couldn't believe her eyes. She'd just been thinking about Michael and here he was. His hair was slightly windblown and, of course, all the sexier for it. He wore a charcoal suit that fit his broad shoulders perfectly. The handkerchief peeking from the coat's breast pocket caught her attention. She'd given it to him, surprised him with it actually when he'd gone for the job interview in Los Angeles. He'd kept it? She'd figured he would have burned every last reminder of their life together.

She dragged her gaze back to his face. A pair of blue eyes smiled along with his mouth. She nearly sighed.

As much as he liked her earlobes, she loved his mouth. He had the best pair of lips she'd ever seen on a man. Wide and decidedly masculine despite being somewhat full. And she was staring at them, she realized.

"What are you doing here?" she asked.

"I'm meeting with a client. What about you?"

"The same."

His gaze narrowed. "That makes me nervous and I think you know why."

"I could say the same thing. A little birdie at Aphrodite's Boudoir mentioned that you were in to see Joanna Clarkson again. You've been busy since losing Rawley."

"I was busy before then." He winked, looking both smug and sexy. Sam wasn't sure whether she wanted to sigh or slap him.

"What floor is your client on?"

"The fifteenth."

"Ah. I'm heading up to the twenty-eighth. Care to share an elevator?" she asked.

"I'll go one better. I'll buy you lunch."

"Picking up the tab again?"

"Yes." His brows arched in challenge. "Are you going to argue about it again?"

She took a moment. "I guess not." And then, because she couldn't resist goading him, Sam added, "If your generosity keeps up I won't feel the least bit guilty about spending such an outrageous sum on the designer heels I bought last week."

"Women and shoes," Michael muttered as they walked toward the bank of elevators with a crowd of other suit-clad professionals. While they waited to board a car, he asked, "How long do you think your appointment will last?"

"I don't know." She shrugged. "Not that long, forty minutes tops."

"Mine shouldn't take more than an hour. We're just going over a couple of proposed changes."

"I'll wait for you in the lobby," Sam told him. "It's such a nice day out, maybe we can dine al fresco."

"This isn't what I had in mind when I said al fresco," Sam said. "And I don't consider this to be a real meal."

They were seated on a bench in Central Park. Michael was two bites away from finishing the hot dog he'd purchased from a vendor. Sam had yet to start hers. Despite her complaints, he was enjoying himself and he was pretty sure she was, too.

It was a gorgeous day despite the breeze, with a cloudless sky and temperatures approaching the seventies. It was far too nice to be cooped up inside a crowded restaurant when Michael would be spending the rest of the afternoon and a good portion of the evening holed up in his office fine-tuning the national print campaign for a client.

"You used to get a craving for a good dog at least once a week. Tony said you helped keep him in business," Michael said of the street vendor they'd frequented.

Sam fussed with the straw sticking out of her can of diet soda. "No one made a dog like Tony. His buns were always so soft." She glanced sideways. "You know what I mean."

"God, I hope so," Michael replied on a chuckle.

She sipped her soda and went on. "I haven't had a hot dog since I moved out of our apartment."

Our. He chased away the nostalgia and regrets the word conjured up by asking, "Why'd you give them up?"

"I prefer to live a long and healthy life. Do you have any idea the kind of stuff they put in these things?"

"No and please don't share it with me now. I'm eating." He popped the last bite into his mouth and chewed contentedly.

"Here you go." She handed over her hot dog, which was still wrapped in foil and warm to the touch. "Help yourself to mine."

"Are you sure you don't want it? A bag of pretzels isn't much of a lunch."

"No, it's not," she replied pointedly. "I plan to order something when I get back to my office. I'm thinking a nice grilled chicken breast on a bed of organic greens. *Mmm.*"

It hadn't sounded all that appetizing until that noise vibrated from the back of her throat. Now, Michael swore his mouth was watering. He swallowed. Yep. Definitely watering.

"Let me guess. Low-fat dressing."

"No dressing at all. A slight drizzle of lemon juice will do."

"You're living large these days, Sam. What will you have for dinner? Bean sprouts and tofu?"

She shook her head. "That's not on the takeout menu."

"When did you turn into such a health nut?"

"I'm not a health nut. I still like a big bowl of triple-fudge ice cream now and then and I'll never give up red meat, even if I do try to eat it less often. I've just been trying to eat healthy, take care of myself."

"That's probably a good idea," he conceded. "You're not getting any younger."

Her lip curled. "Gee, thanks for pointing that out."

"No problem." He grinned.

"As if I could forget with my mother's constant reminders that my biological clock is ticking like a time bomb." Sam's cheeks grew pink after saying so. She popped a pretzel in her mouth and chewed.

"You're not *that* old," he assured her, though the topic of biological clocks made Michael decidedly uncomfortable. "There's still plenty of time for…well, you know."

"They're called children," she said dryly.

"Right." And he and Sam had wanted a couple of them, though they'd planned to wait a few years after marriage before starting their family. If things had worked out between them, would they be parents by now? Something soft and unfamiliar tugged at him, a yearning he didn't quite understand and had never felt before. He cleared his throat and changed the subject.

"Well, if you're eating takeout at your office again tonight it sounds like you've got a long afternoon and evening ahead of you." He reached over to filch one of her pretzels.

She swatted his hand away. "I do. *Very* long. I should have brought a change of clothes for the little time I'll have to sleep tonight before heading back to the office in the morning."

He snorted out a laugh. "I know the feeling. I've been living at Grafton Surry lately."

"Your social life must be as exciting as mine." Her expression sobered, giving him the impression she regretted making such an admission. He, on the other hand, was ridiculously pleased. Not caring to examine why, he decided to goad her.

"Is that a polite way of trying to find out if I have a significant other?"

He expected Sam to take the bait and blow up. She didn't. After taking a lengthy sip of cola, she instead turned toward him and boldly asked, "Well, do you? After the way you've kissed me twice now, I find myself wanting to know."

"No." He shifted so he could place an elbow on the back of the park bench. The breeze caught her hair, tugging it this way and that. Before he could think better of it, he again reached over and tucked some of it behind one ear. The pad of his thumb lingered on her cheek. Her skin was so soft. He pulled his hand back. But it was too late. Now he had to know. "What about you? Any significant others?"

She brushed some pretzel crumbs from her lap. "I think I just made it pretty clear that I'm not seriously involved with anyone."

Yes, she had. And, God help him, Michael liked knowing that. But now her use of the word seriously had him wondering. "Does that mean you're *casually* involved with someone?"

"At the moment, no."

At the moment. Another disturbing caveat that served up another helping of curiosity. Michael opened his mouth to seek further clarification only to have Sam shove a pretzel into it.

Her dark eyes glittered with amusement and challenge when she said, "Unless you're willing to go into detail about your romantic pursuits for the past seven years, I don't think you want to ask me about mine."

"I suppose that's fair," Michael muttered. Though it didn't make him any less curious.

Sam rose to her feet and reached for the jacket she'd removed earlier. "Well, I should get back. The only thing I'm working on here is my tan."

He stood as well. "I got a chance to work on mine during the photo shoot in California."

"I noticed." Sam's smile twisted up his hormones. "See you later, Michael."

CHAPTER SEVEN

WHETHER it was the result of winning the Addy, the loss of the Rawley account or spending time with Sam, during the past several weeks Michael had felt more energized and creative than he had in months, maybe even in years.

He had an appointment with Sidney Dumont set for the following week to pitch his campaign. And it was a good thing, too, since the Herriman rumors had been confirmed in the current issue of *Advertising Age*.

Around the corner from Michael's apartment was a little market that offered a decent selection of meats, produce and freshly baked breads. He wasn't much of a cook, but whenever he grew tired of takeout food and microwavable fare he stopped there on his way home from the office. That was the case on this Thursday evening. But after looking at a neatly trimmed porterhouse steak, he changed his mind.

It was after eight o'clock and the idea of a heavy meal wasn't all that appealing, especially if he not only had to cook it, but eat it alone.

Of course, he didn't have to eat alone. He didn't have to *be* alone. He knew a couple of women who'd made it plain they'd welcome his advances. The one he wanted, though, was Sam, who was eager and reckless one minute and then every bit as cautious and restrained as he was the next.

A habit, he'd called it after they'd kissed. He still hadn't decided if it was the kind he would come to regret. Maybe it was time to find out.

Sam did a double take after glancing through the security hole on her door. What was Michael doing outside? And why did he have to visit when she looked a mess? She'd worked late, as usual. Afterward, she'd felt too keyed up to go home, so she'd gone to the health club to work off excess energy, which she refused to believe might be sexual frustration. She'd overdone it a bit on the weight machines. Her quad muscles felt as if they'd just scaled Everest. So, for the past fifteen minutes, she'd been soaking in a hot bath complete with lavender-scented salts and lighted candles. She considered ignoring his knock and getting back to it, but in the end she pulled the lapels of her terry cloth robe together, sucked in a breath and opened the door.

"I'm catching you at a bad time," Michael said, sounding appropriately apologetic, even as his gaze slipped and his lips curved in male appreciation.

"I was taking a bath," she admitted.

"With bubbles?"

Memories of the things the pair of them used to do in the tub flooded back, but Sam maintained her poise and asked, "Is there any other kind?"

His grin spread. "At last, something we agree on."

She shifted her weight to one foot. "What are you doing here at this time of night, Michael?"

"Would you believe me if I said I was just passing by and decided to drop in?"

"No."

"Okay, how about this. I wanted to see you."

The words had her flesh tingling, but she ignored the sensation. It was late, she was barely clothed, he looked like sin in a suit, and a bottle of wine was peeking from the top of the grocery bag he held. Sam could do the math. Even so, she asked, "Why?"

Instead of answering her question, he coaxed, "Come on, Sam. Invite me in."

No. Sam definitely was not going to invite Michael into her apartment, especially while she was wearing nothing more than terry cloth and he was wearing that grin.

But she heard herself say, "It depends on what you've got in the bag."

"You sure know how to put pressure on a guy," he grumbled good-naturedly.

"You're in advertising, Michael. You're used to pressure."

"I also know the value of presentation and doing

research." He reached into the bag and slowly extracted a loaf of bread. "Italian. Hard crust and made just this morning." His tone was a seductive whisper that stroked each syllable. She found herself swallowing as he added, with a comical bob of his eyebrows, "Best of all, no additives or preservatives."

Sam folded her arms. "All right. Go on. You've got my attention."

He tucked the bread back inside and pulled out a package of herb-coated goat cheese. "This is not exactly low calorie, but you did say the other day that you indulge yourself now and again with ice cream. I figure this is worth a little indulgence, too."

"I've got nothing against treating myself on occasion," she said with a careless shrug.

"Good." His gaze lingered on her lips for a moment. Then, with a flourish of his hand, he extracted the wine from the bag. "And the coup de grace, an award-winning Cabernet Franc that offers a succulent display of berries and silky tannins."

"Did you write the ad copy for that?"

"Nope. I'm just a huge fan of the product."

"Medallion," she said, glancing at the label. "I've heard of them. They're in Michigan, right?"

"Yes, and they took the gold at an international competition with this particular vintage."

"I can't wait to try it."

"Does that mean you're inviting me in?"

Sam stepped back from the doorway and heaved a

sigh, though she was feeling anything but resigned. "Why not? My bath is probably cold by now, anyway."

"Don't be so gracious," she heard him mutter.

After handing Michael a corkscrew and acquainting him with her galley kitchen, Sam went to let the water out of the tub and blow out the candles. Then she changed into blue jeans and a fleece pullover. She resisted the urge to reapply her makeup or fuss with her hair, which had turned curly from the humidity. This was Michael. For six months before their wedding that wasn't they'd lived together. Sam's lease had been up and she'd spent most of her time at Michael's anyway. He'd seen her without makeup or perfectly groomed hair on plenty of occasions.

Sam slid her feet into the fuzzy slippers at the side of her bed and ignored the taunting inner voice that whispered, "He always claimed you were the most beautiful woman on the planet."

When she returned to her living room he was stalking around it. Energy. Michael had always had an endless supply. She'd appreciated that, too. At certain times more than others, she recalled now, as heat spiraled through her body. Fanning her face, she decided the fleece pullover was a bad idea. She felt too warm.

And he looked positively hot. He'd shed his jacket along with his tie. The sleeves of his shirt were rolled up, as if he was eager to get down to some sort of business. Hmm.

Sam cleared her throat. "Are you going to take a seat or would you rather wear a path in my Oriental rug?"

Michael turned around quickly, looking a little startled. Then he went perfectly still.

"Wh-what?"

"You are the only woman I've ever known who looks as good dressed down as she does done up for a night out on the town."

His compliment warmed her far more than she wanted it to. Her heart thumped and then it began to ache as memories shifted to the forefront. To counteract her reaction she forced a note of flippancy into her tone and pointed to the food he'd laid out on a cutting board and placed in the center of her coffee table.

"Flattery won't get you as far as a little bit of goat cheese spread on a thin slice of that bread."

With a half smile, he got to work. When he handed her the bread he asked in a frightfully serious voice, "How far exactly do you want to go, Sam?"

"The balcony," Sam remarked, striving to keep her tone light. "It's a nice night." And she was feeling overheated once again.

After collecting her glass of wine, she exited the room through the pair of French doors on the far end. They opened to a tiny outdoor space lined with planter boxes that were empty at the moment, though she had plans to fill them with annuals soon. In the center stood a bistro table and chairs. She sat on one of the chairs, expecting Michael to take the other one and join her in the light that shone through the doors. He leaned against the railing instead, leaving his face in shadow.

"That's not what I meant, and you know it," he said after taking a sip of his wine.

Sam moistened her lips. "Can we talk about something else?"

"Coward," he said, but he changed the subject. "I like your apartment, by the way. The decor suits you far more than the furniture at your office does." He tilted his head to one side. "Please tell me you didn't pick out that desk."

"No. It was Sonya's. The office was Sonya's. She decorated it."

"And you've kept it exactly as it was. Why?"

She shrugged. "It felt wrong to change things."

"Why?" he persisted.

"You *know* why."

"I know you love your sister and that at one point the job you have was hers and so was the office. Both of them are yours now. They have been for seven years."

"I know exactly how long it's been," she snapped.

"Sorry. Of course you do."

"Just so you know, I'm not rooted in the past. This apartment was hers before the accident, too. After I moved in I changed the window treatments and carpets, repainted the walls and furnished it to my taste."

Our taste, she thought, recalling their studio. She wondered if Michael had noticed that the couch was of the same sleek European styling as the one they'd picked out together.

"But not your office, where, arguably you spend more time," he said. "Are you afraid of what your father would say?"

"No!" But the denial sounded forced, even to her own ears. Could that be the reason? She didn't care to mull it over now. "Can we talk about something else, please?"

"Fine. How about the Herriman account," he asked as he stepped from the shadows.

She blinked in surprise but kept her voice bland. "The Herriman account?"

He chuckled and took the seat across from her. "Come on, Sam. It's in *Advertising Age*. Are you telling me you don't know they're looking for new blood?"

She allowed one side of her mouth to slide upward. "I might have heard something to that effect."

"Are you going for it?"

She sniffed, vaguely insulted. "You have to ask?"

Michael's hearty laughter rang out into the night. "No. I figured as much. Of course, now that the news has been confirmed publicly, every advertising agency in Manhattan and beyond will be gunning for the account, too."

"I'm not afraid of a little competition. So, did you know about it beforehand?" she inquired.

"I've been working on a campaign for weeks."

He looked awfully pleased with himself, which is why Sam said, "I have, too. Ever since Atlanta."

"Atlanta?" That brought him up short as she'd hoped it would.

Sam said nothing. She ran the tip of one index finger around the rim of her wineglass and shrugged.

"You've got a bit of a jump on me, then." Michael let out a whistle.

Straining to keep her smile in check, she inquired, "Are you worried?"

"Maybe just a little. After all, I know what you're capable of, Sam." Though he said it in an offhanded manner, the compliment still warmed her. "But the race doesn't always go to the swiftest."

"True. But I have no problem standing at the finish line waiting for the rest of the pack to catch up with me."

"Does that mean you've already met with Sidney Dumont?" he asked.

She didn't like having to say, "Not yet. I'm waiting to hear back from her."

Sam wished she hadn't put it that way when he grinned. "She can be a bit eccentric when it comes to returning calls, but she did return mine. I've got an appointment on Monday, first thing. I'd offer to put in a good word for you, but that would be counterproductive."

"I don't need a good word," she said stiffly.

"Of course you don't. So, may the best ad exec win?" His brows lifted.

"Yes, and I will."

His laughter was low. "Who knew that arrogance could be such a damned turn-on?"

I did, Sam thought. Even at his cockiest, Michael had managed to get under her skin in a way no other man had ever managed to do. In fact, Michael was doing it now. She sipped her wine.

"Why did you come here tonight, Michael? Surely it wasn't to compare notes on the Herriman account?"

"Do you *want* to compare notes?"

"You know what I mean. So?"

His cockiness vanished. For just a moment he appeared almost vulnerable, but then he stood and walked to the railing. Once again his face was obscured, making it hard for her to gauge his emotions, especially when he said in a conversational tone, "The other night I said kissing you had become a habit. Remember?"

"Yes."

"Nothing about being with you is as mundane as a habit."

"Oh?" It came out a whisper. How she wished she could see his face since she didn't have a clue where he was going with this conversation.

"Uh-uh. It's more lethal than that." He huffed out a breath. "You're like a damned addiction." Finally he stepped into the light. The intensity of his gaze stole her breath, and that was before he said, "I want you."

Even as her heart thumped unsteadily and her pulse began to rev, Sam planned to be casual about his startling confession. But she botched the attempt by dropping her wineglass when she went to set it on the table. The wine splattered. The glass shattered. Michael's expression never wavered.

"I see we're both on the same page," he remarked dryly and lowered himself into the chair.

Were they? She needed to be sure. "Define *want.*"

His gaze turned molten. "I'd rather offer a demonstration."

"Michael, I'm being serious."

"So am I. I want you, Sam." He snorted. "Do I really need to define the word for you?"

She shook her head. "I guess not."

He waited a beat. "Got anything else to add?"

She wanted him, too, though she couldn't quite bring herself to say so. She still recalled the old hurt too vividly. Instead she said, "We had our chance."

"I know, Sam. I keep telling myself that. We came this close to forever." He measured out an inch between his index finger and thumb. "Then we blew it."

We. Though Sam had preferred to blame him fully over the years, she nodded now. We. Yes, it had been a joint effort. She could have called Michael back or gone to see him. She could have tried harder to make him understand.

The fact that she hadn't had her whispering, "Maybe some things just aren't meant to be."

"I've told myself that, too." He scrubbed his hands down his face, looking weary suddenly, where a moment earlier he'd had the energy of a caged tiger. "Maybe that's why I came back to New York, to prove it to myself."

His admission came as a newsflash. So, his uncertainty and lingering feelings for her weren't recent.

"Any luck in that regard?" she asked.

"Yeah," he said with wounding honesty. But then he added, "Until I talked to you after the Addy Awards in Atlanta."

That brought her back to a most salient point. "So much time has passed. So much between us has changed. We're rivals, Michael. We work at competing agencies."

"And you work for your father." It came out not as an accusation, but almost as a regret.

"I have no plans to quit," she told him. They needed to be clear on that.

"I know. You're next in line for the throne," he murmured.

"I've worked hard, Michael. I've earned it." She said it emphatically to quell the worries that her father still might not view it that way.

Michael seemed to read her mind. "I know that you have, Sam. But has Randolph noticed? Has he given you the pat on the back you've been hungering for your entire life? Has he finally looked at you not as a fill-in for Sonya, but as being competent and talented in your own right?"

Anger bubbled to the surface, hot and lethal. God, she wished she hadn't dropped her wine. She'd be throwing it in his face right now.

"It's always been so damned easy for you to judge

me!" she shouted, slashing a hand through the air. "After all these years, how is it possible that you still haven't got a clue? You were born not only with a silver spoon in your mouth, but with a set of doting parents who've tripped over themselves in their praise of your accomplishments and helped you get back up on the occasions when you failed."

He folded his hands on the tabletop and leaned forward. "That's the way it's supposed to work. Parents are supposed to be there for you. They aren't supposed to make you earn their affection. And they're sure as hell not supposed to play favorites."

Her eyes began to sting. "As an only child you know this how?"

"Don't try to cloud the issue with an argument over family size. I was the one who wiped your tears when Randolph kept insisting there were no openings at Bradford for an account executive even though he created a position for Sonya after she graduated. I was the one who suggested a fresh start in Los Angeles where we could both work at the same agency and you wouldn't feel so funny about working for someone other than your dad. You know I'm right."

Yes, she did. So she changed tactics. "You don't have to work."

"Why not? My parents and grandparents worked hard for what they have. I've never felt my inheritance should make me lazy. I knew too many people like that growing up. Besides, my wealth isn't the issue!"

"Maybe not, but since you're having a field day analyzing my motivations and missteps, I'd say a little quid pro quo is in order. Why haven't you started your own agency yet? What's stopping you?

His gaze narrowed and he shifted back in his seat. "You know my reasons, Sam. They haven't changed."

"Yes, yes." She nodded and waved a hand. "But you know what I think? I think all your talk about gaining experience and using only money you've earned on your own is a convenient excuse."

"So what's the real reason?"

"I don't know." She hunched her shoulders, and though it was low, she asked, "Could the mighty Michael Lewis be afraid of failure?"

Her comment didn't get the reaction she expected. He didn't shoot out of his chair and then stomp out of the apartment. No. He regarded her quietly, his brow crinkling as if something had just occurred to him.

"I'm not afraid of failing, Sam. But maybe you're right. Maybe I do have other reasons for dragging my feet."

"Look, it's late. I'm tired and this is old ground. There's really no point in plowing through it a second time." Sam stood and took a step toward the French doors. She had forgotten all about the busted wineglass until a pointy shard of it pierced the thin sole of her slipper and wedged itself in her heel.

"Ow!"

She crumpled back onto the chair, sucking a deep breath in through clenched teeth as she pulled the injured foot onto the opposite knee to inspect the damage. Michael was at her side before she'd removed the slipper. He did the honors for her, taking the glass with it. Blood had already pooled at the wound site. He pulled a handkerchief from his rear pocket and wiped it away.

"I don't think you'll require stitches, but let's get you inside where the light is better and take care of it."

Before Sam could protest, he'd swung her up into his arms. Holding her firmly to his chest, he strode into the apartment.

"It's just a little cut," she objected, though admittedly it hurt like the dickens. "I can take care of it myself."

Michael lowered her onto the couch without saying a word and disappeared down the hall. He returned a moment later with a hand towel, bandages, some cotton balls and a bottle of rubbing alcohol.

"Wh-what do you think you're going to do with that?" Sam asked, pointing at the rubbing alcohol.

"I'm going to disinfect the wound."

"My glass was filled with wine." She picked up the bottle of Cabernet Franc that sat on the coffee table and tapped its label. "Twelve percent alcohol by volume. It says so right here. Under the circumstances, I'd say the use of rubbing alcohol is overkill."

"Germs won't think so." He offered his most charming smile. "And I'd hate to have you lose your foot to some nasty infection because I was remiss."

"I promise not to sue."

"Even a little infection would make it difficult for you to walk." He stopped, shrugged. "Maybe that's not such a bad thing. If you're out of commission you won't be able to go after my clients."

Sam stuck out her foot. "Have at it."

Michael uncapped the bottle and soaked the cotton ball before kneeling in front of her. Cradling her heel in one hand, he said, "This won't hurt…much."

Of course it did. So much so she nearly kicked him in the chin. "God! Are you trying to kill me?"

"You always were such a wimp when it came to pain," he remarked.

"Please. I wear three-inch heels to work every day. I can tolerate…pain…very well." Her thoughts fractured when he began to blow on her foot.

He glanced up, eyes gleaming. "Better?"

"Somewhat." Actually, it was other parts of her that had begun to ache now.

He applied a bandage and she figured that was the end of it. But he kept hold of her foot. "Maybe I should rub your arch so it doesn't feel neglected."

"Knock yourself out." She shrugged though she wanted to purr. How embarrassing would that be? But the man had a great set of hands and he knew how to use them.

Michael didn't just rub her arch. He massaged it,

pressing firmly with his thumbs. She was teetering on the edge of insanity when he leaned over and kissed the spot where his thumbs had been, and she was sent into a freefall. On the way down, Sam was pretty sure she purred.

Chagrinned, she stole a glance at him. He didn't look triumphant or smug. He looked every bit as tortured and turned on as she felt. Heaven help them both.

"Sam." He whispered her name as he set her foot aside, giving him the opportunity to move into the space between her legs. Still kneeling on the floor, he settled his hands on her hips.

"We can't…"

He pulled her forward, to the edge of the couch cushion. Nuzzling her neck, he asked, "Why not?"

"Michael, we're different people now," she began.

"I think so, too. Which, in a way, means we have no history." His mouth was on her shoulder and he was tugging aside the pullover so he could have better access to it. "When you think about it that way, it makes sense."

"No, it doesn't." Of course, nothing was making sense at the moment. "We're going after each other's clients."

"So?" His teeth nipped at her heated skin.

"S-s-so?" she managed to gasp out. "Even without our history, I'd say that makes us rivals."

"In business," he agreed. He gave up on the neckline of her pullover and reached for the hem. His gaze shot to hers. The look in his eyes was challenging, hungry and damned persuasive. "This is pure—"

"Pleasure." She sighed out the word and helped him pull the top over her head.

CHAPTER EIGHT

MICHAEL woke up a few hours before dawn. He considered staying the night. He wanted to and he doubted Sam would object if he did, but he climbed out of bed, dressed quietly in her dark bedroom and, after leaving a note next to the coffeemaker, let himself out of the apartment.

He needed to think and he couldn't do that with Sam's heated body pressed up against his.

The sex had been phenomenal, of course. Better even than he remembered, and that was saying a lot. Despite their mutual hunger and eagerness, they'd taken their time getting reacquainted with one another's bodies. They'd definitely been rewarded for their restraint. But as he made his way back to his apartment in the wee hours of the morning, he thought about Sam's comment about opening an agency.

He wasn't afraid of failing. He had the know-how and he certainly could muster enough clients to kick his business venture off in high gear. Nor was it purely a matter of using his own funds to finance start-up costs, which had been his most handy excuse during the past seven years. No, the fact was, Michael had put it off because he didn't want to do it alone. He wanted a partner.

Back when they'd been engaged, he'd known Sam would be that partner. Though they'd never really talked about it, it had been assumed they'd go into business together. She had such a fine eye for detail. He could always see the big picture. Together they made an excellent team.

After their breakup, Michael still had harbored dreams of becoming his own boss. He'd told himself that just as he didn't need Sam as his wife, he didn't need her professionally. Still he'd found reasons to tread slowly. Now he thought he knew why, and it scared the hell out of him.

Maybe rekindling their relationship wasn't such a good idea. Of course, it wasn't as if he'd proposed marriage again or anything else so serious. But where else was this heading? Casual and Sam were two things he knew didn't mix. They might be able to keep business and pleasure separate and distinct, but could they pick up where they'd left off seven years ago without risking falling in love again? Or hurting each other for the second time? And if the latter occurred, could he survive it?

Sam was woven into every facet of his life, which was why their first breakup still haunted him. How ironic, he thought, that he'd come back to New York with the hope of exorcising the woman from his heart, only to wind up welcoming her back into it.

Of course, certain things were clearer to him now than they were then. Given Sonya's worsened condition, he understood why Sam had stayed in Manhattan. But it also was clear that Sam was still eager for her father's affection and approval.

What if that never changed?

A few hours later, Michael was still struggling to find the answers to his many questions when his cell phone trilled. He'd already showered, shaved and dressed and was on his way to the office after having stopped at the coffee shop on the corner for a bagel and cup of French roast. It was a nice morning, still cool since the sun hadn't made it over the tops of the buildings. Though the distance between his apartment and his office was anything but short, he'd opted to walk.

After juggling his briefcase, the coffee and the bag that held the bagel so that he could answer the phone, he said, "Good morning."

"Is it?" Sam's tone was dubious. "I wouldn't know since I woke up alone."

He pictured her in the big four-poster bed, a cream-colored duvet hiding satiny skin. After swallowing hard, he said, "Sorry about that. I didn't want to disturb you. You were sleeping so peacefully when I got up."

He should have known Sam would see right through his embellishment of the truth.

"You're a liar as well as a coward, Michael." Her tone was curiously conversational, though, leaving him to wonder if she was truly angry with him. "You ducked out on me because you wanted to deal with your morning-after regrets in private."

The silence stretched as he tried to come up with a suitable reply.

"Well?" she nudged.

"I wouldn't call them regrets," he said slowly. "Although I do have some…concerns."

She let out an indelicate snort. "You might have mentioned those *concerns* to me last night before you helped me off with my shirt."

Don't forget the lacy bra, he thought. He certainly hadn't, which was why he stammered, "I…I got caught up in the moment." He sucked in a breath. "It was one hell of a moment."

Her husky laughter came as a relief. "Yes, it was. I guess I got caught up in it, too."

"Twice," he reminded her.

More laughter followed, even huskier than before. "Yeah, well, I was hoping for a third bout with insanity this morning, but your side of the bed was empty."

Michael had reached a corner just as she offered the suggestive comment. Failing to heed the Don't Walk sign, he stepped out into traffic and nearly got run over by a speeding taxi. Its blaring horn and the driver's shouted curse brought him back to his senses.

"It sounds like you're in your car," Sam noted.

At the moment, he wished he was. "Actually, I'm walking down Columbus Avenue. And thanks to your very distracting comment I nearly became a taxi cab's hood ornament."

"Why are you walking and where are you going?"

"You're just full of questions this morning," he said.

"You know me. I always feel chatty after sex."

"Yeah." They used to lie awake for hours, wrapped in each others arms as they shared their dreams and secrets. He diluted that dangerous memory with teasing humor. "Maybe it's a good thing then that we stopped after two rounds between the sheets or you'd never shut up."

"I'm going to forget you said that." But then her tone turned serious. "Instead of telling me where you're going, why don't you tell me where we're headed?"

"I've been trying to figure that out ever since I left your place, Sam."

"And?"

"Just for the record, I'm sorry for leaving this morning without saying goodbye, even if I did kiss you while you were sleeping and leave a note by the coffeepot."

"Thanks for that."

He sighed. "If you were anyone else, this would be simple. We'd spend some time together, get to know each other better. You know, go on dates, talk, fool around a lot."

"Last night you said that since we'd changed so much in the past seven years it meant we didn't really have a history," Sam reminded him.

Michael stopped walking. "I know I said that. But we do, Sam. And it's been front and center in my mind ever since I woke up."

"I see."

"No," he protested. "I don't think you do. After things ended between us, it took me a long time to feel whole again and start living my life solo." Thinking of his stalled agency plans, he finished with, "In fact, I don't know if I really ever have."

It was a hell of an admission, one he'd never thought he'd make, especially to her. It left him feeling exposed, but he needed to be totally honest.

"A piece of me has been missing, too," she replied.

At her words, Michael closed his eyes. God, they were a pair. They couldn't go back, undo the mistakes they'd made in the past. It remained to be seen if they could move forward.

"I'd say we both have a lot at stake."

"Yes," she agreed.

"Why don't we take a few days, do some hard thinking about what we want?" he suggested.

"You mean, look at the situation without the haze of hormones obscuring our vision?"

"Yeah." He chuckled softly.

"That's probably a good idea," she conceded. "In the meantime I have plenty to keep me busy at work, if you know what I mean."

He did indeed. The Herriman account.

* * *

Research. Landing an account as large as Herriman Luxury Hotels required a lot of it. Sam had spent the better part of the past couple of weeks establishing a target market. It had been no easy task since she was doing so without input from anyone at Herriman, but she was comfortable with her conclusions. The chain was known for its high-end amenities and services for wealthy guests, but that didn't mean it couldn't also appeal to business travelers and vacationing families.

The chain had hotels in every major metropolitan area in the United States as well as select cities abroad. Accommodations in several of them were currently being renovated, which, as she sat at her desk late one night, Sam concluded could be the jumping-off point for a new campaign.

She rubbed her weary eyes and tried to envision a television commercial, but thoughts of Michael distracted her. It had been nearly a week since she'd woken up alone after that incredible night of sex. Oddly enough, when she'd glanced over to find the opposite side of the bed empty, she hadn't been angry or hurt as much as curious. What was Michael feeling? So, she'd called him, hoping to ferret out a clue.

After things ended between us, it took me a long time to feel whole again and start living my life solo. In fact, I don't know if I really ever have.

She could still hear him saying the words. They played through her mind at regular intervals. How she wished she could have seen his face when he said them.

Not to determine his sincerity, that had come through loud and clear, but to revel in it.

His honesty had staggered her, which was why she'd agreed to his suggestion that they step back and take time to evaluate the situation before seeing each other again. The idea had seemed so sensible at the time. It was turning out to be pure torture, especially since her body and her mind kept reaching conflicting conclusions.

Her head said take care. This was one flame that might be best left to flicker out completely lest Sam find herself burned beyond any hope of recovery.

Her body said stoke the embers. It will be worth turning to ash to enjoy that hot blast of passion again for however long it lasts.

Was a compromise between those two schools of thought possible? If so, were she and Michael capable of such compromise? Sam didn't know.

She refocused on the computer screen, where her cursor blinked impatiently. She couldn't think of Michael now. Tucking her hair behind her ears, she straightened in her seat and reminded herself that the question she needed to concentrate on was how to get Sidney Dumont to return her calls.

It had been nearly a month since Sam had first contacted Herriman's advertising manager, but she had yet to secure an appointment. In fact, she got the odd feeling Sidney Dumont was purposely snubbing her, which made no sense. The two women had never even met.

Randolph, of course, was breathing down Sam's neck now that news of the hotel chain's quest for a fresh advertising campaign had become common knowledge in industry circles.

Sam remained confident that she had what it took to compete, no matter how many contenders entered the field. She'd spent the lead time she'd had since Atlanta well. She'd pulled together a number of ideas for a first-class multimedia campaign that she felt would meet Herriman's needs, but it would all be for naught if she didn't get the chance to present it.

She was feeling desperate. And desperate times called for desperate measures. So, when she saw the article about the Tempest Herriman-McKinnon Children's Charity Ball on the front of the *New York Times* feature section, she not only read it, she clipped it out.

The ball, which was that Friday, was only in its fifth year, but already had become one of the highlights of the Manhattan social scene. Attendance was limited to five hundred people, making the tickets hard to come by and much sought after, even though they went for a thousand dollars each.

Tempest herself had no direct involvement in her family's hotel business, but she had grown close to her parents now that she was happily married to a U.S. senator and the mother of twins. Surely they—and perhaps key members of the hotel staff—would be there. If Sam got really lucky, perhaps even Sidney

Dumont would be in attendance. It was a long shot, Sam knew. But at this time she was willing to take it.

She shelled out the money for a ticket to the ball without any regrets. She would write it off as a business expense. Not only did the ball attract the mayor and other New York dignitaries, in the past the guest list had included a good number of the city's elite entrepreneurs, who also tended to have the deepest pockets when it came to their business's advertising budgets. One way or another, she planned to get her money's worth.

The first person Michael considered calling when he left Sidney's office was Sam. Not to gloat that the meeting had gone well, but to share his excitement. He'd dialed his parents instead. His father answered.

"Congratulations, son," Drew said, his voice thick with warmth and pride. "I knew you could do it."

"I haven't done anything yet," Michael reminded him. "It was only a preliminary meeting and I'm sure the advertising manager has meetings with at least a couple of other firms scheduled." Bizarrely, he hoped Bradford was one of them. "She said she'll get back with me if they decide they want to go with Grafton Surry. Then we'll really start playing ball."

"Well, I have every confidence in your talent, even if it turns out that the people at Herriman fail to recognize it."

It was Drew's polite way of saying that, win or lose, he would remain proud of Michael. That knowledge warmed him.

"Thanks, Dad."

Michael hung up, smiling until Sam's words of the other evening came back to him. He'd never had reason to question whether his parents were proud of him or wonder if they truly accepted him. She was right about how fortunate he was to have their unwavering love and support. What might Michael do if, like Sam's father, they'd withheld both?

Michael mulled that question over for the next few days, even as he was supposed to be sorting out the current status of their relationship. He still believed Sam should have made a clean break from Randolph when she'd had the chance seven years earlier, Sonya's accident and subsequent health crisis notwithstanding. But had he been fair in demanding it?

The conclusion he reached was humbling. Randolph wasn't the only one to attach strings to his love. Michael had had conditions, too. He'd made their future together contingent on Sam severing ties with her father.

He still wasn't sure where they were heading, but he knew with certainty he wouldn't make that mistake a second time.

CHAPTER NINE

THE week before his meeting with Sidney, Michael had received a personalized note from Tempest Herriman-McKinnon inviting him to her annual Children's Charity Ball at the Manhattan Herriman. That was no surprise. While living in California, Michael had been a generous supporter of Tempest's husband's Senate campaign. He'd also contributed to the many worthwhile causes the hotel-chain-heiress-turned-actress championed. He didn't let the personalized invitation go to his head. She was trying to raise funds, and going to the event meant shelling out a thousand dollars. Still, he considered attending.

Unfortunately, the only woman he wanted to ask to accompany him was Sam. And that was a problem. In addition to the fact that the ball was linked, however loosely, to the account for which they were both vying, he and Sam were supposed to be taking a step back and thinking carefully before seeing each other again.

For that reason Michael decided he would send Tempest a generous donation in lieu of attending. But while he was in Sidney's office for their meeting, he'd noticed a similar personalized note from Tempest in the woman's in-box. Though he generally wasn't one for name-dropping, in this instance it seemed appropriate.

"Are you going, too?" he'd asked and with a smile added, "Tempest can be pretty persuasive."

"You know Tempest?"

"Not well, no. But since I supported her husband's Senate bid as well as some of her pet projects when I lived in California, I'm still on her mailing list." He'd grinned engagingly, turning on what Sam long ago had dubbed the Lewis charm.

"Well, perhaps I'll see you there," Sidney had replied. Then, even though the woman was downright stingy with her smiles, one had lit up her face. "You can buy me a drink."

So now Michael was committed. At the very least he had to put in an appearance. Between now and the time an agency was named, he needed to keep Grafton Surry front and center in Sidney's mind. He just wished he could do so while also enjoying Sam's company.

"Will you be going to see Sonya tonight?" Randolph asked from the doorway to Samantha's office midafternoon the following Friday. "I have some new clothes I want to send."

Sam glanced up from her computer screen a little surprised. Her father always went to see Sonya on Fridays and so she asked, "Why can't you go?"

Randolph tugged at the corners of his mustache, looking uncharacteristically nervous. "Something's come up—a late meeting with a potential client."

"Must be someone important," she mused.

"Oh, it is."

"Well, sorry. But I already have plans for this evening," Sam told him.

"Plans?" Randolph frowned as if the word were foreign to him.

"Yes." When she'd purchased the ticket, she'd debated telling him about going to the ball, but ultimately she'd decided against it. Until she had an actual appointment with Ms. Dumont, she wasn't going to say a thing.

"Can't they be changed?" he demanded irritably. "Sonya will be expecting company tonight. I don't want her to be disappointed."

Despite the guilt that bubbled up and the anger that threatened, Sam remained polite, but firm. "No, Dad. Sorry. I was out to see Sonya twice already this week. I'll visit her tomorrow. If the weather's nice, I'll take her out on the grounds in her wheelchair. She seems to like that."

He grunted, but apparently was mollified. "I'll go Sunday, then."

"Um, Mom will be there."

"God." Divorced nearly two decades and he still could barely tolerate hearing her mentioned. "Did she say when?"

"I think she and Chad are shooting for early afternoon." Chad was the man—the much younger man—Joy had married a few years after leaving Sam's father.

Randolph's upper lip curled beneath his mustache. "I'll visit in the evening." He pointed a finger at Sam. "And I'll see you bright and early on Monday. Don't forget that the staff meeting was moved up two hours. Try to be more prepared this time."

She'd had to run back to her office at last month's meeting for the sales numbers he wanted on one of her clients. He still hadn't let her forget it. "Of course, Dad. Have a good weekend."

Randolph left without bidding her the same.

Michael suppressed the urge to unknot his bow tie. His tuxedo was Armani, but that didn't make it or the sleek black tie he'd paired it with any more comfortable, especially since he felt conspicuous. Not that his attire was inappropriate. The ball was definitely a black-tie affair. But he hated that he was here alone.

His plan for the evening was to locate Sidney, maybe share a drink and some polite conversation, and then discreetly head for the exits immediately after dinner was served. Though he'd heard a big-name band and a couple of Grammy-Award-winning singers were on tap for the entertainment, he wanted to be home in time to catch the last couple of innings of the ball game. The Yankees were playing their arch rivals, the Red Sox, in Boston and it promised to be one hell of a game.

Rivalries always were, he thought, as he turned and caught a glimpse of dark hair and pale skin.

Sam.

Awareness charged up his spine like a stampeding elephant. Sipping his champagne, Michael decided that catching the end of the baseball game wasn't such a big deal, nor was he in a hurry to find Sidney. Grabbing a second flute of bubbly from a passing waiter's tray, he started off in Sam's direction.

"How's your foot?" he asked when he reached her.

She turned and her eyes opened wide. "Michael! What are you—"

"Doing here?" he finished for her. He held out the champagne. "Having a drink with you and inquiring about your sole. The one that ends in *e.*"

She accepted the glass with a smile. "Thank you. As for my foot it's as good as new." She pulled aside the hem of her gown, showing off a strappy sandal the same color as the dress. She'd painted her toenails blood red for the occasion.

After clearing his throat, Michael said, "I'm glad to see that you suffered no lasting effects from your injury."

"None whatsoever. I'm sure it was your careful ministrations that made all the difference in my full recovery. So, thank you."

"Are you referring to the first aid I administered, or what came afterward?" He arched his brows meaningfully.

She ignored the question. "So what are you doing here?"

"I was invited. In the past I've supported Tempest's husband's political ambitions as well as her philanthropic endeavors. Apparently she remembered that and decided to send me a personalized note urging me to attend." He shrugged and came completely clean. "Of course, it's more likely she figured I wouldn't blink at the donation and hoped I might be willing to pony up a bit more."

Sam grinned now. "And have you?"

"Well, it is for a good cause."

"Yes, it is," she agreed. "The after-school program Tempest wants to see expanded throughout New York's boroughs is a proven winner at keeping 'tweens and teens from getting involved in drugs, gangs and sex."

"I see you read the brochure," he said to keep from groaning aloud. Sam looked like sin in a low-plunging sapphire gown and she'd had to go and mention sex.

He took a slow, bracing sip of his champagne, reminding himself of the business at hand. After swallowing, he asked, "So, that's the only reason you shelled out big money to be here tonight? You wanted to support a worthy cause?"

"What other reason would I have?" She smiled sweetly, apparently choosing to keep her cards close to her vest in the high-stakes game they were playing.

Michael opted to up the ante, but only enough to keep things interesting. "Oh, I don't know. I thought maybe you wanted to get an up-close-and-personal view of the Manhattan Herriman and its banquet facilities. They are top of the line and a major selling feature when it comes to conventions."

Sam's lips were painted a ripe shade of red, making her crafty smile a complete turn-on. "Do you really think I haven't already done that, Michael?"

"No. I've done it myself." He decided to toss in all of his chips. "So, maybe the real reason you're here is that you're hoping to catch Sidney Dumont alone, give her a little preview of what the Bradford Agency has to offer and then slip her your business card."

Sam's eyelids flickered in surprise and he figured he'd nailed it. Nonetheless, he gave her high marks for maintaining a bored tone when she replied, "Please, Michael. I wouldn't be as blatant as that."

He glanced over her shoulder and couldn't believe his luck. "That's good to know, because she's coming this way."

Sam barely had time to compose herself before she was face-to-face with the woman she'd been trying to snag a meeting with for more than a month.

"Michael," Sidney said, extending a hand. Though the woman was fifty if she was a day, Sam swore she batted her stubby eyelashes at him. And no wonder. The man did things for a tuxedo that should have been outlawed. "It's good to see you again."

Again. Sam had known they'd already met, but for some reason she seethed at the reminder.

As for Michael, he was oozing charm when he replied, "I was going to say the same." He turned toward Sam then, offering a wink that shouldn't have set off her pulse the way it did, especially given their surroundings. "This is Samantha Bradford. I'm sure you recognize the name. She works for the Bradford Agency. Sam, Sidney Dumont, the advertising manager at Herriman," he added unnecessarily.

"Ms. Dumont, I'm pleased to finally meet you." Sam offered her hand, which the other woman shook less than enthusiastically.

The three of them chatted politely about Tempest's charity for a few minutes, then Sidney made her excuses and left.

"I get the feeling she doesn't like me," Sam murmured as she watched the other woman disappear through the crowd. Turning to Michael, she added, "Which makes absolutely no sense. While I've called her office and left messages, I've never met her before tonight. You don't think she's put off by my persistence, do you?"

Michael was frowning. "I was pretty persistent myself. I had her office number on my speed dial at one point. I can't see where that would be an issue for someone in her position." Then, in a low, seductive voice, he said, "Maybe she's jealous of your beauty."

"And maybe you're full of—"

"Flattery?"

"Other words come to mind, but I guess that will do."

She smiled then, letting her puzzlement over Sidney's demeanor slip to the background. "Speaking of flattery, I suppose it's only fair I tell you how handsome you look this evening."

"Thanks. That's a great dress, by the way. I like what it does for your...waist." His gaze, however, was lingering a little higher than that. "It's by the same designer as the one you wore to the Addy's, I believe."

"You've got a good eye."

"Women's fashion isn't exactly my forte, but I try to pay attention when it's my client's work. So, are you still trying to lure him over to Bradford?" Michael inquired.

Sam shook her head. "I've got bigger fish to fry these days."

That wasn't the only reason, though. It felt wrong to go after Michael's clients if she was only doing so because they were his clients.

He seemed to understand. "I know what you mean." Then he leaned over to whisper in her ear, "You do look lovely."

"Thanks."

"I didn't realize you were going to be here."

"Does the fact that I am complicate matters for you?" she inquired.

"Only a lot." But he smiled after saying so. "The evening promises to be far more interesting now, so that's a plus. I like your hair like that, by the way."

She'd worn it up, sleekly twisted in the back.

Michael had always preferred it off her neck when they went out to formal events, she recalled now. He'd enjoyed the easy access to her nape and, when they were alone, he'd liked taking it down, pin by pin, and then running his fingers through it. Sam swallowed.

"Have you been doing a lot of thinking since we last saw each other?" she asked.

"Probably too much," he admitted. "I made a list of pros and cons the other night when I couldn't sleep. And not sleeping, by the way, has become a regular occurrence."

She knew exactly what he meant. All she seemed to do lately was toss and turn…and yearn. But she merely shrugged. "So, which column had more, the pros or the cons?"

"It was pretty much a tie."

"That's interesting." She sipped her champagne. And though it was a bold-faced lie, she told him, "I did the same thing myself."

"Really?"

"Yeah."

"And?"

She laughed softly. "Same outcome, I'm afraid."

"Should we go for a tie-breaker?" Michael stepped closer, close enough that she could smell his cologne. That masculine scent still lingered on her pillow.

"I don't know." She shrugged. "What will it prove? It shouldn't take a list of pros and cons to determine compatibility."

"No. There are other, more interactive ways to do that," he whispered suggestively into her ear, causing her to shiver.

Even though Sam wanted to move forward, she took a step back. "I believe we've already determined that we're more than compatible in that regard. That's one of the reasons we decided not to see each other for a while. It's hard to think when all you want to do is get naked."

"Did you have to put it like that? The mental image is…" He closed his eyes and groaned.

"Sorry." And she was. Michael wasn't the only one getting wound up. "Maybe we should talk about other things."

"Yes. Please. Although, let me say, we were good together, Sam. And I'm not just talking about in the bedroom."

She smiled and, as promised, changed the subject.

"I probably shouldn't ask this, but I've been dying to know. How did your meeting with Sidney go?"

"Well, I probably shouldn't tell you this, but it went well." It wasn't arrogance that lit up his eyes. It was excitement as he offered the highlights. "I wanted to call you afterward, just because I knew you'd understand how pumped up I was." He sobered then. "Hell, Sam, I've wanted to call more than just then. I've picked up the phone at least a dozen times with the intention of dialing your number."

"But you haven't."

"No." He unbuttoned his tuxedo jacket and tucked his free hand into the front pocket of his trousers. "What about you? Have you been tempted to call me?"

"Not in the least. I've wanted to *see* you," she admitted to him. To herself she added, and touch you, make love to you.

"And here I am." The carnal edge to his smile made her wonder if he'd been reading her mind.

"Did you come alone?"

"There was no one else I wanted to bring." Something behind Sam snagged Michael's attention then and his expression changed from turned on to ticked off. "I see you didn't have that problem."

Sam followed the direction of Michael's gaze. Just inside the entrance to the Grand Ballroom stood her father.

"What's he doing here?" she hissed.

Michael's attention snapped back to her. "You didn't know he was coming?"

"No. He said he had a late meeting with…a potential client," she finished as the edges of her vision turned red.

Her father was decked out in formal wear and already working the room like the professional he was, shaking hands, slapping backs and making introductions with Roger Louten, one of Bradford's newest account executives, at his side. When he spied Sam, Randolph's thousand-watt smile dimmed. Did he feel guilty at being caught or was he merely annoyed? At the moment Sam didn't really care.

She saw him lean over to say something to Roger, apparently excusing himself. A moment later he joined her and Michael.

"Hello, Samantha."

Randolph pointedly ignored Michael, who took a step back and said, "I'll go find us a couple of seats."

When they were alone, her father demanded in a hushed tone, "What are you doing here?"

"I guess you could say I have a late meeting with a potential client," she replied, parroting his earlier words. "I think we both know who that potential client is. How could you go behind my back this way, Dad?"

"I haven't gone behind your back. I'm just offering a little assistance. We work on the same team, remember. Michael Lewis is the one you have to watch out for."

She didn't see it that way. Michael might be her rival, but he respected her talents far more than her father did. Indeed, if they were talking adversaries, Sam considered Roger a bigger one than Michael ever was. "Why is Roger here, Dad? You think I need help landing this account so you bring in someone who's been with our agency all of a year?"

"It's not like that." But he glanced away, tugged on his mustache, leaving Sam with the sinking certainty that it was exactly like that. "He's a smart young man, if a little green. I thought you both might benefit from working together on this account."

"When were you going to mention this to me?"

But then she shook her head. "No, what I really want to know is, how long ago did you make this decision?"

"I've had Roger working on it for a couple of weeks now. You weren't getting anywhere, Sam."

It took an effort to maintain her composure. Her voice rose only a little as she replied, "I beg to differ! I've spent hours researching the market and spent late nights working up a creative strategy."

"That's your strength," Randolph agreed, throwing her a bone. "Roger, however, is more aggressive than you are. He's made several contacts with Sidney's people."

She expelled a breath and in a dry tone said, "And yet we're both here tonight trying to get a few minutes of her time. It doesn't appear that wonder boy is all that wonderful, and I'm not sharing my account with him. I don't care if we're on the same team or not."

"This isn't your call."

She crossed her arms. "It should be and you know it." In the hope that he would see reason, she pointed out for a second time, "I'm the one who first heard the rumors and followed up on them. I've done the research, spent hours on it as a matter of fact. You know that, since you've dogged me every step of the way."

"I'm sorry, Sam. We can't afford to let an account of this size slip to a competitor."

"And you have so little faith in my ability after my seven years at Bradford that you think I'd allow that to happen?"

"It's not personal," he said.

Would he offer that same excuse if in the end he handed over the reins of the agency to someone else? "It is, Dad. It's completely personal. You've never believed in me. Not when I was twelve or twenty or even now that I'm in my thirties. Sonya could do no wrong as far as you were concerned and I still can't get anything right."

"Sam, please." He rolled his eyes. "Now is not the time for female histrionics or family squabbles."

She chose to ignore the female histrionics comment, but not the other. "When is the time for family disagreements? We rarely socialize outside of work, Dad. When you get right down to it, our relationship is far more professional than it is personal."

"You've been listening to Lewis again," he accused. "He's always been eager to turn you against me."

"Do you really think he's had to try? You've managed that all on your own."

"Don't push it, Sam."

"Or what? You'll disown me? You'll *fire* me?" She expelled a liberating breath. "Aren't they one and the same thing where our relationship is concerned?"

Randolph's jaw clenched. She expected an explosion. Instead he said, "Let's mind the matter at hand and leave this for another time. I see that Roger has already managed to engage Ms. Dumont in conversation."

He sounded so triumphant that Sam had to say, "I've talked to Sidney tonight, too. I was introduced to her just before you arrived."

Randolph's eyes narrowed, but at least she had his full attention. "And?"

Although it was an utter embellishment of the truth, Sam said, "She promised me a moment of her time later this evening." She gestured toward Roger, who apparently was receiving the same cool reception and quick dismissal Sam had earlier. "It doesn't appear she appreciates having another Bradford representative stalking her between now and then."

Randolph nodded begrudgingly. "Roger and I will leave after dinner. But you'd better have something concrete to show for tonight or changes may be in order."

She resented the warning. Even more, she hated that it had her stomach knotting with the same dread she'd always experienced as a child. "Of course," she said just as Michael returned.

Turning to her father, she said a little awkwardly, "You remember Michael."

"Only too well," Randolph muttered as his gaze slid to the side. Not surprisingly, he failed to offer a hand.

Michael took his rudeness in stride. "Hello, Randolph. It's been a while."

"Not long enough. And I prefer that you call me Mr. Bradford," came her father's stony reply.

"Gee, and to think that at one time I was all set to call you Dad."

Sam felt her lips twitch as her father's face turned an unbecoming shade of purple. Michael and her father had never gotten along, and it had irked Randolph to no end that he'd been unable to intimidate the younger man.

He turned to Sam. "If you're really serious about the matter we just discussed, Samantha, you'd better think twice about the company you keep."

Her mirth of a moment ago evaporated. "I have."

"Good." Randolph flashed a smile at Michael. "Roger and I will save you a place at our table."

"That won't be necessary." She pushed her arm through Michael's. "I have other plans. I'll see you Monday morning."

CHAPTER TEN

MICHAEL didn't say anything as he escorted Sam to the seats he'd found for them at a table near the stage. Even though he was pleased and a little surprised by the way she'd just stood up to her father, he didn't think she'd appreciate hearing him say so at the moment. She looked wound tight enough to explode.

A couple of other people were already seated at their table. They introduced themselves, chatted briefly, as was only polite. Once they were settled in their seats, he told her, "I took the liberty of getting you another glass of champagne."

"I could use something a little stronger than that," she muttered.

"What would you like?" When he started to rise, she stopped him by laying a hand on his arm.

"That's okay, Michael. I need to keep a clear head." She huffed out a breath, looking both angry and perplexed when she added, "Suddenly everything seems to be riding on tonight."

"What do you mean?"

"Never mind."

"So you didn't know Randolph was coming," he remarked casually.

"No. Of course, I kept him in the dark about my plans, too."

"Why?"

She shook her head, as if to signal an end to the questioning, but then she admitted, "Dad's been fly-specking my every move ever since I told him about Herriman. He's always badgering me for an update and when I don't have anything new to report, which lately I haven't, he's..." Sam sighed.

She didn't have to finish. Michael knew just how unreasonable and demanding her father could be, especially when it came to his younger daughter.

"So, who's the guy he brought with him?"

"Apparently, competition," she grumbled.

"What?"

She shook her head. "Forget it."

When she remained silent, Michael coaxed, "Come on. You can talk to me, Sam. Friend to friend."

Sam turned sideways in her chair and faced him fully. "Is that what we are, Michael? Friends?"

A pair of dark eyes brimmed with other, more specific questions regarding their relationship. He had answers for her. Suddenly, he had answers for himself, but now was neither the right time nor place. So he offered a trimmed-down version of the truth.

"We're also a lot more than friends, and I'm not referring to anything to do with our careers."

She closed her eyes and sighed. "It doesn't matter anyway. Here I've been worried about you and it turns out that my biggest adversary is in the office three doors down the hall."

"The guy with your father," he surmised.

"Roger Louten," she spat out the name. "He's a young and very hungry account executive. Dad hired him fresh from college barely a year ago, and I just found out that he's been working on the Herriman account behind my back. Dad tried to pass it off as wanting me to act as a mentor. You know, help season the new kid. But that doesn't change the fact that my father is treating me like an inexperienced rookie."

Michael seethed for her at the insult. Sam was so damned talented and creative. Her campaigns were nothing shy of brilliant. If her peers in the industry recognized that, why couldn't her father?

"What an ass," he mumbled.

"Who? Roger, Randolph or me?" Her laughter was laced with disgust. "And I had to go and inflate the truth, make it sound like Sidney has agreed to talk to me this evening."

"The night's young. You can make that happen." He didn't stop to question why he hoped that Sam got her chance. Suddenly calling the Herriman account his wasn't as important as seeing Sam happy and confident again.

"God, I hope so."

Because she sounded so glum, he said, "Even if it doesn't, it's not the end of the world. Call her office first thing Monday and go from there."

"Monday will be too late. You're right about my father, Michael. You've always been right."

He knew that, of course, but it pained him to see her so miserable, so damned defeated. "I'm sorry, Sam. For what it's worth, I don't want to be right." When her eyes grew bright and he saw her swallow, his own throat ached. "Don't, Sam," he whispered hoarsely and reached for her hand. "Don't cry."

She blinked rapidly and worked up a smile, rallying in a way that made Michael proud of her and eager to go a few rounds in a boxing ring, gloves optional, with Randolph.

"Thanks." She squeezed his hand, laced her fingers through his. "If nothing else good comes of tonight, at least I got to dance with you."

Michael blinked in confusion. "Did I miss something? The music hasn't started yet."

"No, but when it does I know you'll ask me."

"I will," he promised. Not only because Samantha Bradford was a hard woman to resist, but because Michael no longer wanted to.

They dined on mixed baby greens drizzled in a light vinaigrette, grilled salmon served on a bed of asparagus risotto and tender green beans topped with sliced almonds. Though the food was first class, Sam merely picked at it. Michael understood completely her lack of appetite. But when dessert arrived, she perked up considerably. It was a rich chocolate layer cake topped with a fresh raspberry sauce and chocolate shavings.

"Appetite coming back?" he asked, as she nipped off a corner with her fork.

"It's chocolate, Michael. I'd have to be dead not to eat chocolate." She eyed his cake. "Are you going to eat that?"

"Yeah. But I could be persuaded to share."

"How so?"

"I'll tell you later."

And he did, while they danced, holding Sam close and whispering a suggestion in her ear that made them both eager to call it an evening. First, though, Sam needed to speak to Sidney.

Michael walked the perimeter of the room while Sam went to the ladies' room to freshen up. Sidney actually found him.

"I couldn't help but notice how cozy you were with Samantha Bradford on the dance floor," she remarked. "I find that rather interesting considering that you're both after the same thing."

Yes, they were. And it had nothing to do with advertising, he thought. But he said, "Business is business."

"Yes."

"You don't seem to like her," he commented. "Or maybe I'm reading you wrong."

"You're not reading me wrong. I don't like pushy advertising execs who step over boundaries. The Bradford Agency seems to be full of them. Her father accosted my assistant at the gym, got him to confirm that we were looking for new blood before I was ready to do so publicly. Now tonight, both she and another young man from their agency have approached me."

"Sam didn't approach you," he felt compelled to point out. "Actually, you approached the two of us and I introduced you. Work was never mentioned."

Sidney let out an indelicate snort. "Yes, but it's a good bet it would have been, given the number of times she's called my office in the past few weeks."

"Can I ask why you haven't returned her calls?"

"Call it an idiosyncrasy of mine," Sidney said with a wave of her hand. "I spend nearly seventy hours in my office each week. When I leave for the day, I prefer not to discuss work unless it's with my employer. I certainly don't appreciate having my assistant ambushed after hours."

"So you've blackballed the Bradford Agency," he said.

"Yes."

"That's a shame."

"A shame?" Sidney eyed him in surprise. "I should think that news would make you happy. I plan to make my decision soon and there are already enough hats in the ring. Don't you want to come out on top?"

"I like to be the best," Michael said slowly. "To that end I prefer to compete against the best."

Her eyes narrowed. "You're saying Samantha Bradford is so good you wouldn't mind losing to her."

"Oh, I'd mind," he corrected. "But I'd know the best campaign won."

"With all of the other advertising executives out there, you assume that one or the other of you is the best?"

"That's right," he agreed with a nod.

"You're cocky, Michael." But Sidney chuckled.

"I've been told that before. I like to think of myself as confident."

"Yes, well, for all that I still like you." Sidney tilted her head to one side. "Does Samantha Bradford know how much you love her?"

Michael swallowed. That obvious, he thought? He didn't care. Shaking his head, he said, "I don't think so, but I'm planning to remedy that soon."

Sidney laughed. "You do realize that yours is going to be a complicated relationship given your jobs?"

"Yes." But life without Sam had its own set of complications. He'd prefer her in it, and they could work out whatever problems arose, even if she forgave Randolph again and decided to stay at his agency.

Over Sidney's shoulder, he spied Sam. She was heading their way, no doubt preparing to offer a subtle pitch. Given what he'd just learned, he had to stop her. Otherwise she would blow what little chance she had of getting her foot in the door.

"Will you excuse me?"

"Of course." Glancing in Sam's direction, Sidney said, "Tell her to call my office on Monday. First thing after lunch."

He blinked in surprise. "Really?"

"I'm not promising anything," the woman warned. "But I'll talk to her. After all, while she's been tenacious, she's also been the least offensive one from her agency to approach me. Perhaps I've been unfair."

"Thanks."

Sidney waved her hand in dismissal. "Fools," he thought he heard her mutter as he walked away.

"Sam." Michael reached for her arm, stopping her in her tracks a dozen feet from where Sidney stood. "I have to talk to you."

"In a minute."

"Now."

She glanced up at him. "Can't it wait, Michael? Sidney is right there. And she's alone."

"I know. That's what I need to talk to you about. Please."

"But—"

"Trust me," he said.

He experienced relief and something far deeper when Sam nodded and let him lead her to a quiet corner of the room.

"I was talking to Sidney and she mentioned how much she hates being approached in public about work. Apparently, she's especially irritated with your father for 'accosting' her assistant, and that's a quote."

"That would explain the cold shoulder she's been giving me."

"Yes."

"So talking to her now would be the kiss of death." Sam closed her eyes and let out a sigh. "Great. She won't return my calls and the one time I see her I can't talk to her about business."

He squeezed her arm. "Call her Monday."

"Why? What difference will it make?" Sam asked.

"Call her." He smiled and for a second time said, "Trust me, okay?"

"What did you do, Michael?"

He shrugged. "I just told her the truth. That you're one of the best in the business."

Sam swallowed. "You did that? For me? Why?"

A number of reasons came to mind. The one he offered was, "When I beat you, I want it to be fair and square."

The phone rang first thing the following morning. Sam had to wriggle from beneath Michael's heavy arm to reach for it.

Into the receiver she offered a sleepy, "Hello."

"What happened after Roger and I left last night?"

It was her father. Apparently, he'd decided he couldn't wait until Monday morning to get a report.

"What time is it?" she mumbled, pushing the hair out of her eyes so she could squint at the clock. It was barely 8:00 a.m.

"Never mind the time," he said impatiently. "Did you talk to Sidney last night? What did she say?"

"I…I'm to call her Monday."

"And?" Randolph pressed.

"There is no and. I imagine she'll let me know then if she wants to set up an appointment."

"That's all?" His disappointment came through loud and clear.

"That's more than Roger has managed while working behind my back," she snapped. "And by the way, Dad, it turns out that Sidney is a little peeved with you for approaching her assistant at the gym and tricking him into confirming the rumors. That's why she hasn't returned any of my calls. I'm lucky she's agreed to speak to me at all."

She glanced at Michael, who had begun to stir. Lucky, she thought again, when his eyes opened and his lips curved in irresistible invitation.

"Well, all that is water under the bridge now," Randolph was saying. "We'll get together first thing Monday and you, Roger and I can—"

Whatever else her father was about to say was lost as Sam hung up the phone.

"Good morning," she told Michael.

"Yeah." Pulling her close, he murmured against her neck, "I know a way to make it even better."

CHAPTER ELEVEN

Sam was smiling when she arrived at the Bradford Agency bright and early Monday. She and Michael had spent the entire weekend together, visiting with Sonya on Saturday, after which they'd enjoyed a quiet dinner in her apartment. As for Sunday, they'd spent most of it in bed talking, reading, watching old movies and making love.

In addition to showing Sam how much he loved her, Michael had said the words, quietly, passionately and with the hint of a promise.

This morning, before they'd each headed off to their respective places of work, he'd kissed her soundly before hailing her a cab.

"Good luck."

"Same to you," she'd said.

"Dinner tonight?"

"Yes. And let's eat in again." She'd grinned, he'd groaned and all had been right with the world…until she walked into her office half an hour later.

Randolph was in the chair behind her desk, peering at the screen of her computer, which had been booted up. Roger was sifting through some mock-ups that Sam had had the art department prepare the previous week.

"What's going on? What are you doing in here?" she demanded, setting her attaché case aside.

"We're just doing some prep work for your meeting with Sidney. I expected you to be in earlier," Randolph said, his tone censorious.

"It's only eight o'clock. And I don't have a meeting with Sidney." Yet, she added silently. "She said to call her after lunch."

"Have a seat. Between now and then I want you to become acquainted with some of the ideas Roger has and work them into your campaign."

"Work them into—" Sam was seething. She was furious and ready to blow. She inhaled deeply, trying to employ the breathing technique she'd relied on in the past to help her relax. Instead of expelling the breath slowly, she let it whoosh out along with a couple of choice expletives. She didn't want to relax.

"Absolutely not! I have a clear vision for Herriman Hotels. If I get the account and once I've met with the Herriman people, if *they* decide they want something different than what I have to offer, then *and only then,*" she stressed, "will I make changes."

"There's no *i* in teamwork, Sam," Roger intoned at the same time her father said, "Be reasonable."

"Being reasonable hasn't gotten me very far with

you, Dad." She crossed her arms. A couple of ultima-
tums came to mind. She opted to keep the more perma-
nent one in reserve. "I do this my way or I don't make
the call. Since she won't take one from either of you,
think carefully before making your decision."

For the rest of the morning, Sam remained closeted
in her office, going over the data from the market
research department, Herriman's current advertising
strategy and paring down her pitch enough to pique
Sidney's curiosity.

It was five minutes past one o'clock when she
reached for the phone and with a shaking finger dialed
the advertising manager's number. When the receptionist put her right through Sam nearly sighed, but
then Sidney was on the other end of the line.

"Samantha, hello."

"Hello and thank you for taking my call."

"You've been pretty persistent," Sidney said coolly.

It wasn't exactly what Sam wanted to hear. She
cleared her throat and fingered the sheaf of papers
before her on the desk blotter. "Yes. Well, I know you're
a busy woman so I'll try to make this as brief as possible, while also keeping it irresistible. Quite obviously,
the Bradford Agency wants your account. And I think
we can offer you an effective multimedia campaign
unlike anything you'll get elsewhere."

It was as far as she got before Sidney stopped her.
"I'm sorry. I don't want to waste any more of your time
or mine. We've already made a decision."

"A decision," Sam repeated dully.

"Yes. Goodbye."

Sam hung up the phone in a daze. What had just happened here? She was still trying to figure that out when Randolph barged into her office a little later.

"I don't get it. Why would she agree to talk to you and then make a decision before even taking your call? Instead of acting as if you were on a date with Lewis, you should have given her something to whet her appetite on Friday. God!" he thundered. "I can't believe you let an account this large just slip away." He shook his head in disgust as he stalked about the room, muttering other comments under his breath. Finally, his anger spent, he asked, "What agency did they go with?"

"I don't know."

"Most likely Grafton Surry," Randolph sneered. "Michael is probably out celebrating even as we speak. Hell, he probably had the account all sewn up on Friday and let Sidney string you along."

"No. Michael would have no reason to do that."

"Revenge," Randolph replied. "I told you that once, and you wouldn't listen."

Revenge. That wasn't what Michael was after.

"He wouldn't do that," she said. But might he have told Sam to call Monday rather than risk having her pique Sidney's interest at the ball, especially if he knew the Herriman people would be making a decision soon?

No, she told herself. Absolutely not. But doubts niggled, growing more insistent when she hadn't heard from him by late afternoon. Sam considered calling him, but in the end decided this was a conversation that needed to occur face to face.

She'd never been to the offices of Grafton Surry. She barely noticed the tasteful furnishings and artwork now as she followed the receptionist to the one where Michael sat behind a desk.

"Hey, Sam. I take it you heard the news about Herriman?" he said when they were alone. His phone began to ring, but he ignored it.

"Yes, I did. I got it from the horse's mouth, so to speak, when I called Sidney."

"Oh. That stinks."

"Yeah." She tilted her head to one side and studied him. "I'm surprised you didn't call after you got word."

"I wanted to, but I've been tied up in a meeting. This is the first break I've had all afternoon."

I bet, she thought. But then she reminded herself not to jump to conclusions. The pledge lasted only until the receptionist poked her head around the door a moment later to inform him, "I have Sidney Dumont on the line, Mr. Lewis. She said she needs to speak to you again."

Michael blinked and Sam gave him high marks for managing to act so surprised. Where her father's betrayals hurt, this one cut to the bone.

"My God, Michael. I can't believe you did this."

"What are you talking about?"

She shoved the hair back from her face. "Offering that tripe about Sidney not liking to be approached outside of work and then getting me to wait to talk to her until today when you knew damned well it would be too late."

"I knew no such thing. I was just as surprised as you when she called to say they'd made a decision."

She shook her head in disgust. "What was it you said that night when I asked you why you would encourage Sidney to hear me out? That you wanted to beat me fair and square. And to think I believed you."

"I didn't lie, Sam." He reached for arm, but she tugged it away. "Why would I lie?"

"I think I've already spelled it out."

"You're not making sense."

"No, Michael. I'm finally done letting my emotions run my life and rule my career."

Michael wasn't sure what had just happened. All he knew was that he didn't understand any of it. He hadn't lied about anything and he sure as hell hadn't set Sam up for failure.

Glancing up, he realized the receptionist and Russ were standing in the same doorway through which Sam had just exited. The receptionist looked embarrassed to have overheard the private exchange. Russ looked livid.

"Miss Dumont on line one," the young woman reminded him before turning to leave.

"I want to see you immediately after you hang up," Russ barked ominously.

"Sidney, hello. Calling back to tell me you made a mistake and want to go with Grafton Surry?"

She chuckled. "Sorry. Actually, it occurred to me that when we spoke earlier I should have apologized about Samantha Bradford. I told you to have her call, but then we wound up moving more quickly than I anticipated."

"I figured that out."

"Anyway, I'm sorry. For what it's worth, I think it's probably a good thing that neither of you got the account, given how hungry you both were for it."

Michael thanked her and hung up. He doubted Sam would agree, especially since at the moment she thought Michael had bested her. She'd know better, of course, if she had allowed him a chance to tell his side of things. But no, she'd jumped to the wrong and unflattering conclusion that he'd cheated. Michael's anger spiked, but then, just as quickly, it ebbed. He had a choice to make. He could simmer in his own self-righteousness and let her walk out of his life as he had done seven years ago or he could go after her and try to put things right.

Back then they'd both been too hard-headed to compromise. He didn't intend to let miscommunication stand between them a second time.

Michael was on his way to the elevator when he remembered Russ and made what he hoped would be a quick detour to his supervisor's office. When he left Grafton Surry two hours later, it was with the boxed-up belongings from his desk and a supreme sense of satisfaction.

* * *

Sam glanced through the peep hole and clenched her teeth. She'd have to have a word with the doorman about letting just anyone up.

"Come on, Sam," Michael hollered. "I know you're in there. I've already been to your office."

It was only out of deference to her neighbors that she opened the door the width of the security chain and, glaring, informed him, "Then you know that I no longer work there."

"I heard that, yes. Was it because of what happened with the Herriman account?"

"The Herriman account was the last straw of many," she replied.

"I'm sorry, Sam." Michael shook his head. "I can't believe he fired you."

"You think I was fired?" Her laughter was brittle. "I quit."

She enjoyed watching Michael's mouth fall open. When he recovered from his surprise, he asked slowly, "How do you feel about that?"

"Good." She nodded for emphasis when she added, "Great, in fact, even though he threatened to disown me. You know, that's when it struck me. To disown somebody you have to own them first. And when you own somebody they're a possession, not a person."

Michael's expression turned soft. "Come on, Sam. Let me in so we can talk."

"What more is there to say? Congratulations?"

He shrugged. "If you really want to offer those, you'll have to call William Daniels at Quest Advertising."

"What?" she asked, sure she'd heard him wrong.

"He got the account." Michael shook his head, looking chagrined. "I'd sure as hell like to know what he offered that was better than what I did."

Sam slammed the door in his face, but only to undo the chain and fling it back open. "I thought you got it."

"Yes." He rubbed his chin. "I realized that when you were standing in my office making all sorts of wild accusations and refusing to listen to my side of the story."

"I...but you...and then Sidney...oh." Sam decided it was best to stop talking.

"You're kind of cute when you're in the wrong." He tipped up her chin with his index finger and dropped a kiss on her lips. "And I have to say, I never thought I'd see the day you were rendered all but speechless."

"You're enjoying this?" Her bafflement was real. She'd accused him of horrible things, yet here he was at her door making light of it.

"I wouldn't say I'm enjoying it, exactly. Do you know why I came here, Sam?"

She wasn't sure of anything at the moment, except that she owed him one huge apology, so she shook her head.

"I came here because seven years ago I was the one jumping to all the wrong conclusions and failing to let you explain. That bit of stupidity cost me dearly."

"Michael—"

He laid his fingers over her lips. "Let me finish, Sam. This needs to be said. I don't know how I got through the past seven years of my life without you. I did, but only because I was too proud and too pig-headed to call you back and try to work things out."

"I could have done that, too," she said. "We're both at fault."

"I know that. Don't think I'm letting you off the hook completely, sweetheart, either then or now," he said with a grin, but then his expression sobered. "It's just that this time, I decided that no matter who was the one jumping to conclusions, I wasn't going to risk losing you again. So here I am, on your door-step." She watched him swallow. "Are you going to let me in?"

Tears spilled down Sam's cheeks as she reached for him and pulled him inside. With her cheek pressed against his, she whispered, "I love you, Michael."

"I love you, too."

Though they'd made love just that morning, when they did so now much had changed. *They* had changed, Sam realized, both of them breaking free of the past.

She sighed contentedly as she lay next to Michael and the shadows grew long in her bedroom.

"So, what are you going to do now?" Michael asked.

"I was thinking about ordering takeout. I'm starving and I want to keep up my strength."

His laughter shook the bed. "I second that idea, but I was talking about your job."

"Ah. Do you know if Grafton Surry is hiring?" she asked.

He levered up on one elbow. "As a matter of fact, they are."

"Great. Maybe you can put in a good word for me. It might be nice for us both to work at the same agency for a change."

"I was thinking the same thing." He grinned, but left her confused when he said, "But that won't happen at Grafton Surry."

"Why not?"

"I don't work there any longer."

"What?" She sat up, causing the covers to fall away from her breasts. When Michael's gaze lowered, Sam poked his bare chest. "Focus, Lewis."

"I am."

"On the conversation," she said dryly. "You were saying?"

"I quit today, too."

"You quit?"

"Resigned. It sounds nicer and you know how I am about phrasing."

"But why? What happened?"

"Russ was irritated as hell when he overheard you mention that I talked to Sidney on your behalf. Before he could launch into a lecture that I truly didn't want to hear, I explained a few pertinent facts to him."

"Such as?"

"One, I didn't like working under his supervision. Two, I didn't like working under anyone's supervision. I've talked about starting my own agency for a long time now."

"You mentioned that you shared a few pertinent facts. What was the third?"

"That I love you."

"You told Russ you loved him?"

He laughed, pulled her toward him. "You know what I mean."

"Yeah."

"And I told him that you and I were going into business together."

Sam pulled back. "You…that's what you want?"

"I do. You're too good. I can't let you work for someone else."

The sincerity in his voice touched her deeply. "Oh, Michael."

"So, how does Lewis and Bradford sound to you?"

"It sounds wonderful, and almost as good as Bradford and Lewis."

"It was my idea."

"Bradford comes before Lewis in the alphabet."

"True." He nuzzled her neck just below her ear and began to work his way down.

When she caught her breath, Sam asked, "So, it's settled?"

His head lifted and he smiled. "I've got a better idea. How about Lewis and Lewis?"

Her heart did a crazy roll. "As in Samantha Lewis and Michael Lewis?"

"You just have to have top billing, don't you?" But he chuckled. "So, is that yes?"

"It's better than yes."

In the dwindling light, he squinted at her. "What's better than yes?"

Pushing him down on the mattress, Sam said, "Let me show you."

0109 Gen Std HB

MILLS & BOON
Pure reading pleasure

FEBRUARY 2009 HARDBACK TITLES

ROMANCE

The Spanish Billionaire's Pregnant Wife	Lynne Graham
The Italian's Ruthless Marriage Command	Helen Bianchin
The Brunelli Baby Bargain	Kim Lawrence
The French Tycoon's Pregnant Mistress	Abby Green
Forced Wife, Royal Love-Child	Trish Morey
The Rich Man's Blackmailed Mistress	Robyn Donald
Pregnant with the De Rossi Heir	Maggie Cox
The British Billionaire's Innocent Bride	Susanne James
The Timber Baron's Virgin Bride	Daphne Clair
The Magnate's Marriage Demand	Robyn Grady
Diamond in the Rough	Diana Palmer
Secret Baby, Surprise Parents	Liz Fielding
The Rebel King	Melissa James
Nine-to-Five Bride	Jennie Adams
Marrying the Manhattan Millionaire	Jackie Braun
The Cowboy and the Princess	Myrna Mackenzie
The Midwife and the Single Dad	Gill Sanderson
The Playboy Firefighter's Proposal	Emily Forbes

HISTORICAL

The Disgraceful Mr Ravenhurst	Louise Allen
The Duke's Cinderella Bride	Carole Mortimer
Impoverished Miss, Convenient Wife	Michelle Styles

MEDICAL™

A Family For His Tiny Twins	Josie Metcalfe
One Night with Her Boss	Alison Roberts
Top-Notch Doc, Outback Bride	Melanie Milburne
A Baby for the Village Doctor	Abigail Gordon

MILLS & BOON®
Pure reading pleasure™

FEBRUARY 2009 LARGE PRINT TITLES

ROMANCE

Virgin for the Billionaire's Taking	Penny Jordan
Purchased: His Perfect Wife	Helen Bianchin
The Vásquez Mistress	Sarah Morgan
At the Sheikh's Bidding	Chantelle Shaw
Bride at Briar's Ridge	Margaret Way
Last-Minute Proposal	Jessica Hart
The Single Mum and the Tycoon	Caroline Anderson
Found: His Royal Baby	Raye Morgan

HISTORICAL

Scandalising the Ton	Diane Gaston
Her Cinderella Season	Deb Marlowe
The Warrior's Princess Bride	Meriel Fuller

MEDICAL™

Their Miracle Baby	Caroline Anderson
The Children's Doctor and the Single Mum	Lilian Darcy
The Spanish Doctor's Love-Child	Kate Hardy
Pregnant Nurse, New-Found Family	Lynne Marshall
Her Very Special Boss	Anne Fraser
The GP's Marriage Wish	Judy Campbell

0209 Gen Std HB

® ™ MILLS & BOON®
Pure reading pleasure™

MARCH 2009 HARDBACK TITLES

ROMANCE

The Sicilian Boss's Mistress	Penny Jordan
Pregnant with the Billionaire's Baby	Carole Mortimer
The Venadicci Marriage Vengeance	Melanie Milburne
The Ruthless Billionaire's Virgin	Susan Stephens
Capelli's Captive Virgin	Sarah Morgan
Savas' Defiant Mistress	Anne McAllister
The Greek Millionaire's Secret Child	Catherine Spencer
Blackmailed Bride, Innocent Wife	Annie West
Pirate Tycoon, Forbidden Baby	Janette Kenny
Kept by Her Greek Boss	Kathryn Ross
Italian Tycoon, Secret Son	Lucy Gordon
Adopted: Family in a Million	Barbara McMahon
The Billionaire's Baby	Nicola Marsh
Blind-Date Baby	Fiona Harper
Hired: Nanny Bride	Cara Colter
Doorstep Daddy	Shirley Jump
The Baby Doctor's Bride	Jessica Matthews
A Mother For His Twins	Lucy Clark

HISTORICAL

Lord Braybrook's Penniless Bride	Elizabeth Rolls
A Country Miss in Hanover Square	Anne Herries
Chosen for the Marriage Bed	Anne O'Brien

MEDICAL™

The Surgeon She's Been Waiting For	Joanna Neil
The Midwife's New-found Family	Fiona McArthur
The Emergency Doctor Claims His Wife	Margaret McDonagh
The Surgeon's Special Delivery	Fiona Lowe

0209 Gen Std LP

MILLS & BOON

Pure reading pleasure™

MARCH 2009 LARGE PRINT TITLES

ROMANCE

Ruthlessly Bedded by the Italian Billionaire	Emma Darcy
Mendez's Mistress	Anne Mather
Rafael's Suitable Bride	Cathy Williams
Desert Prince, Defiant Virgin	Kim Lawrence
Wedded in a Whirlwind	Liz Fielding
Blind Date with the Boss	Barbara Hannay
The Tycoon's Christmas Proposal	Jackie Braun
Christmas Wishes, Mistletoe Kisses	Fiona Harper

HISTORICAL

Scandalous Secret, Defiant Bride	Helen Dickson
A Question of Impropriety	Michelle Styles
Conquering Knight, Captive Lady	Anne O'Brien

MEDICAL™

Sheikh Surgeon Claims His Bride	Josie Metcalfe
A Proposal Worth Waiting For	Lilian Darcy
A Doctor, A Nurse: A Little Miracle	Carol Marinelli
Top-Notch Surgeon, Pregnant Nurse	Amy Andrews
A Mother for His Son	Gill Sanderson
The Playboy Doctor's Marriage Proposal	Fiona Lowe